One of the Family

Maggie Ford was born in the East End of London but at the age of six she moved to Essex, where she lived for the rest of her life. After the death of her first husband, when she was only 26, she went to work as a legal secretary until she remarried in 1968. She had a son and two daughters, all married; her second husband died in 1984. She wrote short stories from the early 1970s, also writing under the name Elizabeth Lord, and continued to publish books up to her death at the age of 92 in 2020.

Also by Maggie Ford

A Brighter Tomorrow
A Fall from Grace
A New Dream

The Lett Family Sagas

One of the Family
Affairs of the Heart
Echoes of the Past

Maggie
FORD
One of the Family

CANELO

First published in Great Britain in 2000 by Severn House Publishers LTD

This edition published in the United Kingdom in 2022 by

Canelo
Unit 9, 5th Floor
Cargo Works, 1-2 Hatfields
London, SE1 9PG
United Kingdom

A CIP catalogue record for this book is available from the British Library.

Print ISBN 978 1 80032 800 6
Ebook ISBN 978 1 80032 438 1

Originally published as *Butterfly Summers* by Elizabeth Lord

Look for more great books at www.canelo.co

Printed and bound in Great Britain by Clays Ltd, Elcograf S.p.A.

1

One

Sometime in the night Henry James Adair Lett died – in the comfort of his own bed surrounded by rich maroon drapes, olive furnishings and all the beautiful *objets d'art* he had collected over the years.

His physician, Dr Jameson, put the time of death at around three o'clock, announcing it to have probably been in his sleep, and reflecting aloud, "Quite the best way to go," for all that Henry Lett was only fifty-five.

He had been discovered around seven o'clock by one of the staff who had brought up his usual morning tea. Marjory, his second wife, twenty years younger than he – his first had died five years earlier – was hurriedly informed, they having separate bedrooms because of his heart condition. His incessant smoking – a habit he had acquired as a young man prior to the First World War – had contributed to that problem and had proved a folly in finishing him off at fifty-five. Marjory immediately telephoned the doctor, the few relatives her husband possessed, and the family solicitor, who held her husband's Last Will and Testament.

The following day, with the deceased installed in the parlour of a firm of funeral directors, his relatives, his one close friend and his two permanent staff – others usually got from an agency if and when needed – gathered at Swift House, his home at Halstead Green in Essex with its three acres of grounds, to settle themselves around the huge dining-table while his solicitor, Mr Benjamin Raymond, sorted out his papers in preparation to reading the will.

"We'll miss him," Sheila Hurshell whispered, blinking away tears. "I know *I* shall."

Her mother, the deceased's sister Victoria, only surviving member of the immediate family now – his other sister Maud no longer alive, her two daughters married on the other side of the world, Henry's brother Geoffrey and his wife killed in the war by a VI rocket, leaving one son – gave a shrug.

"Had good innings, I'd say." She kept her voice down. "He had a very successful life. One of the best restaurants in London. Head of the whole thing after first your grandmother, then your Uncle Geoffrey died. All the big names went there before the war. Not so now. Place gone downhill. And to think, him marrying again after your Aunt Grace died. To a woman half his age. Yes, I say he had good innings."

"He was only fifty-five, Mummy. He should have lasted a lot longer."

"All that smoking. His doctor warned him. Anyway, when it's my turn, I wouldn't complain about going like him." The solicitor was rustling papers, leaning his ear towards something being whispered at him by his clerk bending over him. Victoria took advantage of the moment to enlarge on her potted philosophy, ignoring her husband's dig, a hint that she should be quiet and attentive.

"I mean, he's died the best time for anyone to die. November, one of the most miserable months of the year. Had the best of the summer. Doesn't have to look forward to a dreary winter like the rest of us. Went in the best possible way too, after a hearty dinner, his usual cigar and a nightcap. He must have had some sense of well-being when he went to bed. Two or three hours' sound sleep before going like that. The doctor said he couldn't even have been aware he'd gone. He wouldn't have felt any fear of the unknown. I suppose had he been aware he was about to pop off, *that* would have been a bit of upsetting—"

"Will you shut up!"

Victoria drew a offended breath through her nose as her husband's harsh whisper hissed at her.

"Can't stop rabbiting, can you? Not even here?"

Mr Raymond cleared his throat. The whispering faded. The spacious dining-room, almost sacrilegiously bright for this occasion despite the drawn pale green drapes, became hung with a waiting silence seeming to emphasise a faint stale reek of cigar smoke that lingered regardless of air fresheners, as if the very walls had soaked it up so that an over-imaginative soul might feel the man still here.

Benjamin Raymond glanced around the table.

"I apologise for the delay, ladies and gentlemen. We were waiting for the deceased's son. I have now been told he has arrived."

His eyes took in those present: the deceased's wife; his sister; her husband and daughter; the deceased's nephew Edwin, only son of his brother; the housekeeper; the manservant Pool; and William Goodridge, his restaurant manager, close friend and confidant for thirty-five years. Eight people – when the deceased's son finally made an appearance, nine. Not a large gathering for one who was so successful in business – or who had been at one time, the man in later years a very private person, unlike his brother Geoffrey.

Henry and Geoffrey Lett had inherited their father's business around 1920, Letts Oyster Bar as it had once been known handed down to James Lett from his father who'd received it from his, he having begun with a barrow around 1830 before acquiring premises just off Haymarket, at that time a twice-weekly market for cattle and sheep, hay and straw. The oyster bar had proved a magnet for hungry traders, oysters in those days constituting a cheap meal. The business thriving, it moved on to two other locations before settling just off Jermyn Street. Although it was failing a bit now, in the forward-looking desperation of a badly knocked-about post-war London – Henry Lett had insisted on clinging to

4

old-fashioned values and had not really moved with the times – it was still one of the haunts of the rich and famous.

Noisy footsteps interrupted the solicitor's flow of thought. A voice unnecessarily noisy and hearty invaded the room, and the young man – a youthful version of his late father, or perhaps more his late uncle – burst in through the door.

"Sorry I'm late, folks. Got held up around Hampton Court. They've got a road up. Damned long queue – seems like everyone in England's got a car these days. Anyway, hope I haven't held anyone up."

"You have. Come and sit down, Hugh," his stepmother shot at him, but as he took his seat he gave her a look that said he wasn't a child to be remonstrated with, nor was she his real mother with any right to do so.

Mr Raymond cleared his throat to help combat this brief display of animosity. He was aware that though there existed a long-standing dislike of each other, one aspect stepmother and stepson did share was that, since both expected to be vastly better off under the will, neither wanted involvement with the deceased's presently declining business. Mr Raymond guessed that whichever became the majority share-holder would sell and be rid of the encumbrance. The wife was young – thirty-five. Henry Lett had been smitten by her, feeling the loss of his first wife, and his wealth had created a shining path before her feet. Now Henry Lett was dead and Mr Raymond half suspected Marjory Lett had an admirer lurking somewhere. She wouldoff at the first decent opportunity, she and the money Henry would leave to her. She had no wish to be burdened by a failing business that could collapse and take all her money with it.

Hugh – professional name Hugh Derwent – deemed himself a budding Shakespearean actor, having enjoyed quite a few small parts in several of the Bard's major tragedies. Seeing himself in a leading role within the next few years, he had absolutely no interest in his father's plebeian restaurant business, even less so now that it was going downhill. His eyes were set on grander horizons. He too would sell the shares he was confident of inheriting – he and his stepmother were in agreement on that one. Then, each with their haul, they could go their separate ways.

Pity. Letts still had a lot to offer; in the right hands would rise again, phoenix-like, from the embers of the fine reputation in which it had basked during the years between the wars – its heyday, one might say. But as far as he was aware, Mr Raymond could see that not one of those around this table was willing or interested in carrying Letts on; each wealthy in his own way, none caring to inherit an ailing restaurant, only the shares Henry had left, and then they too would go in with the widow or the son and take their cut.

Mr Raymond cleared his throat again and began reading, inwardly amused by each reaction, the tiny satisfied sigh or the disappointed sniff.

–

"I expect you're feeling quite happy with your little windfall," Edwin Lett remarked to William Goodridge as they were handed their coats in the hall, the other beneficiaries beginning to split up in readiness to leave, the two staff named in the will already back on duty, eyes bright at their small gifts.

Edwin's remark was made kindly and was taken in that vein, the fifty-seven-year-old restaurant manager nodding sociably.

"I am, Mr Lett. Very pleased. Your uncle and I became good friends with the passing years, even though he was my employer. He was that kind of man. I remember him in the old days, coming into the business after his father died late in 1920. I'd been there eighteen months, starting as a mere *debarrasseur*. I left the army at twenty-two after the first war, came out without a scratch and found work straight away – luckier than the poor blighters who'd copped one and couldn't get any job. But I couldn't get promoted very far. It was your uncle who gave me a chance. He was about two years younger than me. I'm sure he didn't know what he was doing. But he seemed to have faith in me, perhaps because we were so close in years, neither of us sure of ourselves. He'd been in the war too, a captain. But he had no side to him. We often had a drink together in one of the pubs around the corner in London."

A girl was coming in through the main door, her coat pulled round her against the cold November air outside. The sight of her turned Edwin's gaze. He had only been half listening to Goodridge's reminiscences, his mind more on the way Hugh and his stepmother had got their heads together after Hugh's first shock of the wife having been given the controlling share of the business instead of him. They had agreed quite amicably, probably for the first time ever, that the business would go, and the others, including himself, were now faced with either selling their shares or hanging on to see who would buy it. Now Edwin forgot to think about it, his gaze concentrated on the young girl. She was stunning – tall, her fair hair loose about her shoulders, her hazel eyes the largest he had even seen, with a figure slim enough for a model's. She looked to be about twenty-four, two years younger than he.

Her wide lips parted in a bright smile. "I've got the car outside. Are you ready, Dad?"

"Just about." Seeing his companion's eyes go from concentrating on the girl to glancing questioningly back at him, William Goodridge's elderly features creased in an amused grin. "Helen, my daughter. Helen, this is Henry Lett's nephew, Edwin. Helen dear, you go ahead, keep the car warm. I'll follow you out. Won't be a moment."

As she turned away, treating Edwin to her wide smile, her father's grin grew wistful. "Helen is our one and only child; I was thirty-three when she came to town. She looks so like her mother sometimes."

Edwin was still gazing after his daughter and seemed not to have heard him. William's eyes glazed a little, remembering a tall girl in a faded coat and ragged tam-o'-shanter, her face peaked with hunger, hanging around the kitchen door at the back of Letts. Under the wretched pallor of poor food she too had been beautiful. Her eyes had been hazel also, and very wide as she implored to be given work, no matter how menial. Mr Samson, the chef, a large, loud, bull-headed man, had been all for kicking her out but Will had been so struck by what he saw under all that deprivation, he had taken pity on her, or been smitten by her – he wasn't sure after all these years what it had been – and had pleaded for her to be given a job of washing-up…

"Well, I'd best be off."

The voice broke through William's thoughts, start-ling him back to the present. "Yes, me too." They struggled into their coats. "Are you going to sell your shares now?" he asked Edwin Lett on a sudden impulse.

"I suppose so," came the absent reply. They moved together towards the large main door with its porti-coed frontage. "A bit sad though. I know the whole thing's going down, but it's a shame to see something die."

9

"You think so?" Hope rang in William's tone. "You know it could still be saved if—"

"No hope," Edwin cut in, surveying the November mist that lay across the gardens beyond the open door. In London it would be thick yellow fog, spoken of these days as smog, because of all the smoke it held suspended in it. "It's had its day. My uncle refused to change with the times and this is his reward. He'd turn in his grave if he knew."

"He's not buried yet," reminded William, a little sternly.

Edwin gave a small apologetic grimace, then attempted to make light of the error. "Well then, he'd turn in the funeral parlour if he knew."

"That he would," agreed William. "He put his life into that place. It was a wonderful place, right up to the war and all through it. It's only since 1947 that it's gone down. But you wouldn't know about the old days, you just a young boy in the thirties. I could tell you some tales."

—

Edwin Lett felt a little annoyed – well, not annoyed exactly. Sad. Yes, he'd been willing enough to sell his shares in agreement with the rest of the family. They all knew that trying to keep Letts going in its present old-fashioned state would be like rolling a granite rock uphill. Any attempt at modernising it would take up a lot of time and money, and no one, including himself, fancied spending *their* time and money on it. It had had its day, and his step-aunt, now holding the majority share, had been approached by two people eager to buy the business, one offer too good to refuse though made by a company who intended changing the name to bring it under the umbrella of their own business.

She had called a meeting and they had all agreed: cash in hand was far better than a failing restaurant. But the name of Letts would die, and that was Edwin's regret. He felt sentimental. He'd liked his uncle, who'd worked all his life keeping that name going. Letts was still one of the best known oyster and fish restaurants in London. Members of Parliament came there, the lesser royals on occasion, stars of stage and screen – though maybe not the great film names of yesterday – and they liked the outdated decor, the atmosphere. But it no longer thrived as it had done in years gone by, those years between the wars that old William Goodridge had described briefly as they'd left that day after the reading of Uncle Henry's will.

Edwin sat by the telephone, one hand lying on it, his mind indecisive. Should he ring William Goodridge? What would he say to him? That he was selling his shares and that Goodridge ought to sell his while he had the chance? But that wasn't the reason he would lift the receiver and dial the number on the piece of paper in his hand. There was another reason.

"We could discuss it in my local," William had suggested over the phone.

Uncertain why a pub rather than a quiet restaurant or his own flat or even Goodridge's home, Edwin had agreed. Perhaps Goodridge felt more at ease in his own local. Now they were sitting together at a small, unsteady, black-painted bentwood table in this dark panelled pub, William with a pint of bitter, he with a double Scotch which at this moment he felt he needed.

Unloading his dilemma on to the man was proving disconcerting. Edwin was having to raise his voice uncomfortably over the Tuesday lunchtime hubbub of drinkers. This wasn't his world. He moved in a world of night-clubs, he and his friends, the grand circle or a box at the theatre or opera, Ascot royal enclosure or the stands at Goodwood; tennis clubs; private house parties, always with a girl on his arm, often looking up old service chums, all of them, like him, ex-army officers.

Since being demobbed he'd enjoyed a lot of time on his hands to decide what to do with his life but so far he had done nothing, unable to make up his mind. He was pretty well off with the house and money that had come to him on his parents' death. There was no need to work. Yet work was the staff of life. Without it, life was nothing, vacant, or had became so of late. With the pleasure of freedom after army restriction at last starting to rub off, he had begun to feel he should be doing *something* with his life.

But why choose Goodridge to unload these problems on? Why need to confide in him, a mere friend of Uncle Henry, of all people? Why not his own friends?

He knew why. None of them would feel as he was feeling at this moment. None of them would put themselves in his shoes; they would merely laugh, shrug, and mutter, "It's up to you, old boy, what you do."

There was something about William Goodridge, something solid and dependable. One felt any words issuing forth from that square mouth set in that square jaw beneath the large nose, grey deep-set eyes and thick greying eyebrows would be words of wisdom and experience, well thought out. Even the way the man was contemplating his pint glass of beer instilled a sense of trust. Edwin took a fortifying swig of his whisky.

"This meeting my family had. They're all for selling the business and having done with it. None of them wants the burden of it. Neither do I, I suppose. It'd cost the earth to bring it up to date. Anyhow, there's been two interests. One is offering silly money though they say they're happy to keep the name going. The other is far more attractive and it does let everyone off the hook. They all see the business as a weight around their necks. The only trouble is the people want to drop our name and use theirs. Nor are they a particularly high-class establishment. A sort of mediocre waitress service, a self-service area for office workers' lunches so I am told, and even sandwiches for taking away. Bloody uncivilised way of eating."

He saw William nod in agreement. He was a man of a time when it had been considered civilised to sit down to meals amid quiet surroundings, such fare as fish and chips served in newspaper reserved for the lower classes unless a company of fellows felt like going out slumming. That of course had been before the war, Edwin a child then. He sipped his Scotch more slowly.

"Mrs Lett said it was a way out for the whole family. She pointed out to us that we all have our own money and don't really need some ailing, old-fashioned restaurant."

He referred to his uncle's widow in formal terms not so much because Goodridge wasn't family but because Edwin had never been able to call the second Mrs Lett "Aunt". That had been and always would be reserved for his uncle's first wife, Grace, whose memory his uncle had appeared to put aside hardly three years after her death for a woman half his age. Hardly able to call her Marjory, he managed to sidestep by not addressing her at all if that was possible, though luckily he saw her seldom so it wasn't hard.

"I admit I was in agreement with the rest of them until I learned the name would be lost. I know things have to change. But seeing my father and my grandfather's name die... That's why I want to talk to you, Mr Goodridge." He paused, not knowing quite what it he wanted to say. "I take it you've a few shares. Will you be selling?"

"Will you?" the man countered quietly, seemingly mesmerised by the pale amber colour of his half-consumed pint of bitter.

"It is a tempting offer. You might be wise to take advantage of it, Mr Goodridge, while it's going."

"It sounds as if you'd be glad if I did. I suppose it'd help my bank balance, as I'll be out of a job. A bit late changing jobs at my time of life." He chuckled. "Let's say you'd probably feel less guilty about your part in seeing the name go if I did sell. Though my few shares wouldn't make much of a hole, would they? I expect you'd stand to make quite a decent profit out of the deal."

For some reason Edwin could not feel irked by the statement, spoken without any trace of bias. Goodridge seemed to know him better than he knew himself. "I expect I would," he said slowly.

Around him the noise of drinkers seemed to grow louder, so that he had to raise his voice when he'd have preferred to use a more confidential tone. Why had Goodridge chosen this of all places to talk? "But I already have all I need to live on."

An only child, he had inherited everything on his parents' death: their shares in the business, their fine home in High Ongar way out in Essex, and the luxury flat here which they'd used occasionally when in London, but to him these days more than just a *pied-a-terre*, comfortable and convenient.

The thought, as it always did, brought back that day in July 1944 when he'd been told of their death, killed by a V1 rocket, a direct hit on a restaurant in Piccadilly. Unfortunately for them they had not been dining in Letts, which remained unscathed a street or two away. He had been just seventeen. Informed by telegram, he'd been sent home from his college, his Aunt Grace hugging him tearfully while his Uncle Henry had set about clearing up all the family matters.

Resolutely Edwin shook off the memory.

"It's still not enough to make an argument of. It boils down to the wishes of my uncle's widow and his son. Little I can do. I ought to sell before the shares become worthless. The same goes for you, Mr Goodridge."

William, who had also been miles away with his own memories, came back to himself, picked up his glass and took a long slow swig, his Adam's apple bobbing like a cork behind the loose skin of his thin neck.

"But you don't want to see the name disappear." He spoke the words as a statement, adding, "It seems to me that is something you are feeling a pressing need to consider. Has it occurred to you that if you feel that strongly about it you would put all you had –

and I think with what you've inherited from your parents you could put in a great deal – into buying out your uncle's widow and his son, so taking control and keeping the restaurant going?"

Edwin was beginning to feel a little rattled. It was none of the man's business what he had. But the man was warming to his subject. "No bank would hesitate to support you for all you'd need. A safe enough investment with the property you've already got."

Safe investment, yes, but did he want to risk so much? Did he even want to do it just for a name? And even more money would be needed to bring the place up to scratch to suit the new age being envisaged by post-war Britain.

"It's too much of a risk."

William Goodridge smiled into his glass. "So you weren't serious after all about not wanting your father and grandfather's great name to die."

Edwin sat silent, stung by what seemed like an accusation. Talking to the old restaurant manager had solved nothing. Yet maybe the older man was correct about his not being serious. To risk all out of mere sentimentality, maybe get into debt, for what? To cling to a name? That was mad. What he wanted to do now was drink up and take his leave of the man who seemed secretly interested only in keeping his position – a highly attractive position, not easy to find elsewhere at his age. But that was unjust. Like himself, the man felt nostalgia, nothing more. Still, it left a nasty taste in his mouth about himself.

He sought to lighten the moment and turned his mind to William Goodridge's daughter. The recollection brought a deep, even pleasurable thumping to his chest. The more he thought of her, the brisk way she had entered the hall of Swift House, the smile she had offered him as they were introduced, those clear hazel eyes and her fair, loosely waving hair, the harder his heart hammered. He was sure that her smile had conveyed a similar interest in him.

Seizing the chance, he asked, for lack of a better excuse to bring up her name, "Did you say Helen was your only child?" He tried to ignore the amused smile that broke out on the other's face.

"That was what I said."

Edwin nodded, already debating as to how he might work around to asking Helen Goodridge for a date. So intent did he become on thinking about it that the man's voice recounting how he had met her mother seemed to recede into the distance, lost amid the countless other conversations going on in the pub.

William Goodridge too had become oblivious of his audience. His eyes glazed to all that was going on around him, his ears closed to the noise. He was seeing another time, hearing other sounds. A restaurant filled with diners, the polite clatter of cutlery against crockery and the tinkle of spoons against coffee cups; the muted chatter of social conversation over good food, fine wine. On a dais a small group of musicians was playing the popular songs of the day – not too imposing as yet. A few venturous couples were on the small dance floor.

As the evening advanced the music would become more lively, the dancers grow more energetic.

Like gorgeously arrayed butterflies, they would flit back and forth across the dance floor, arms raised in a Charleston like wings, the men in black tie and tails and white shirts, the women all shimmering colour.

Butterflies in summer. How many summers before winter came? He remembered too, very clearly, how it was when winter came.

He saw it all again, those two decades between the wars, happy for some, less so for others. And they were the carefree and the famous, those who came to dine at Letts, the famous and the notorious, the stars of film and theatre with their wives, their girl-friends, their mistresses; the titled and the politicians, the eminent rich and those who'd made their pile by less savoury means. He'd got to know something of their lives over the years – their fears, their hopes, their troubles, and something of their private lives, some of it told to him by others, the rest confided in person as he climbed the ladder of his particular occu-pation and came to be trusted. Showing a sympathy and understanding they all recognised, he'd become a sort of confessor figure. Yes, he'd known their secrets, developing an ability to see into their hearts – had a bent for it he supposed. As he'd said earlier to Edwin, he could have told some tales, noble and unsavoury. There had been more than a few questionable characters dining at Letts over the years.

There had been some memorable moments. One memorable moment that had figured greatly in his life. It had been just before Christmas 1919. A Tuesday evening, one of the quieter days of the week, the evening Mary had crept into his life, a waif of eighteen who had captured his young heart – not quite then, precisely, on thinking about it now, but… well, he wasn't quite sure when, but she had.

Two

She stood at the half-open delivery door, the stiff December breeze seeming to blow right through her, so frail she looked; thinly clad, around eighteen, though with a face so pinched by cold it was hard to tell. As with all who suffer poverty, her expression seemed as old as the hills.

The tip of her nose pink from cold, displaying a tiny dewdrop which she wiped away with a swift brush of the back of her hand across it, she gazed in through the open back door of the restaurant, to savour the warmth of its vast kitchen as much as its appetising aromas.

Fred Dodds, one of the scullery staff, looked up from swishing plates through grey soapy water, the addition of a good handful of soda to which made sure of cleaning plates properly and reddening hands completely raw at the same time, and saw the girl standing there. His reaction was immediate. "Wot you want, then? Gern – sling yer 'ook, you."

His rough Cockney attracted the attention of the *chef de cuisine*, undisputed despot of his domain. "Enough of that!" he commanded. "If you can't speak the king's English proper, then don't speak at all. It puts me teeth on edge."

About to berate the lad further, he saw the object of attention and his eyes hardened towards the creature loitering, stubborn from desperation, in the doorway. His vigilance over his large staff interrupted, he growled, "Go away, girl! We've no free feeds here, if that's what you're looking for."

Her voice was faint but adamant. "I'm looking for work. I can work."

"You?" Samson's chuckle gurgled in his throat with sarcasm. It was a chuckle none in his kitchen dared at their peril to assume to be humorous. Chef had no humour. To his mind jokes had no place here. Work only was required, and few laughed in his presence, much less idled their time.

The sizeable restaurant demanding a sizeable kitchen staff, there were thirty-odd employees answerable to him at any one time: *sous chefs*; *chefs de partie*, all with assistants; *commis chefs*; *rotisseurs*; the *garde manger*, again with his assistants; grill cooks, staff cooks, carvers, porters, *aboyeurs* who passed orders between the serving staff and kitchen brigade, at other times acting as Samson's secretary, and many more as well as the young lads who scraped and peeled vegetables or, like Dodds, spent their days with hands in suds washing down work counters and stovetops, washing up plates, cutlery and utensils, and scraping pots with wire wool and elbow grease. The place rang with noise from it all, and over it Samson reigned supreme – in control of all the finances, hiring, firing, menus, ordering, training, organising, and the thousand other things required of a head chef, the least of which was preparing a dish himself unless special circumstances called for it. A man of enviable talents, he'd been with Letts, one of the finest restaurants in London, from apprentice days, slowly climbing the ladder to head chef these fifteen years. Heavily built, his fingers would come to life over some exquisite culinary delicacy with all the grace of a prima ballerina – a joy to see yet, as with any prima ballerina, firm and concise with no hint of indecision. Should he wish to move something from one spot to another, finished dish or mere teaspoon, it was done with panache and it was more than one was worth to touch it until ordered.

He brushed his hands together after having put the finishing touches to a fine salmon mousse which he had been deftly decorating, and directed his ominous, throaty chuckle at the hungry-looking girl standing at the back door of the restaurant.

"Can't work here, girl. You need strong arms to work here. You look half starved to me. No use in this kitchen."

"She c'n 'elp me, Chef," Dodds offered bravely. "Since we lorst our uwer scullery boy, I can't keep up wiv it all. I niver knew a place ter get so busy. Couldn't she fill in—"

"And expect Mr Lett to pay her a wage? Certainly not. We can get help anywhere these days at the drop of a hat, and stronger arms to boot."

It wasn't quite true. Men who'd survived the French and Belgian trenches had come home to a strange situation. There were jobs but few fit young men to fill them. For those who had lost limbs or were paralysed, those blinded or with lungs ruined by poison gases, those chronically sick from all they had endured in the trenches or in German and Turkish prisoner-of-war camps, there were few jobs. So while there were jobs, often ones offering high wages, the streets saw men without work, many of them with no roof but for the temporary shelter of Salvation Army doss-houses, unable to afford the rent for even one damp room. Any who could play an instrument did so, their shoes worn through from shambling along the kerbsides. Others sold matches, pipe-cleaners or shoelaces from rough wooden trays slung from a piece of string about the neck. War widows and their orphans often stood in doorways selling hair clips, pieces of ribbon, bits of lace. Thirteen months after the war's end, people were becoming hardened to them, even irritated by the ill-clothed boys and girls of little more than ten or eleven with hands like birds' claws held out for a penny, a halfpenny, even a farthing to be dropped into them. A heel-end of rock-hard loaf or a bone thrown into a bin from a cafe was a feast. A fire kindled from old bits of wood and straw in some back alley was hub to a circle of crouched figures, a drop of alcohol in a cast-off bottle cause for a free-for-all, a kick on the arse from a bobby pounding his beat often their reward for being there at all.

The girl was just another of them, considered a "scrounger", the term uttered to ease the conscience of the more fortunate.

Dodds was different. He too had known hunger, was deeply grateful for the job he had. "We don't 'ave ter pay 'er, Chef, do we? We c'n just give 'er somefink ter eat for 'er work."

"And be in trouble with the law for making a slave of her? Not likely. Now get along with you, girl. And you, Dodds, get on with your work and don't be so bloody cheeky or you'll be out on your ear too."

William Goodridge came in on the scene as Dodds returned to his swishing of dishes and scrubbing of pans and Samson moved to shoo the intruder away. It was a bit of job, she reluctant to go, ready to dodge any blow aimed at her while still clinging to the hope that the large corpulent man who made four of her would relent – and, William assumed, seeing her thin frame, throw her a crust of bread just to be rid of her.

He put the tray of dirty dishes he bore on to a counter and paused over the serving dish of vegetables awaiting him. He worked here as a *commis de rang*, clearing used plates and bringing vegetables to diners. He saw the girl flinch as Samson's hand flashed out, missing her by inches. But she stood her ground, her eyes a clear hazel, full of challenge. She had spirit. Adversity had obviously not bowed her head as yet. And beneath those grubby cheeks she was appealingly pretty.

On an impulse, William picked up a slice of bread from a plate on the tray he had brought into the kitchen and made towards the girl, holding it out to her. "Here. Take this."

For answer she put her hand behind her back. "I didn't come here for food," she said sharply. "I came for a job. Keep your bread!"

With that she turned and walked off. Chef shot his gaze back to the *commis*. "What d'you do that for, you fool?" he exploded, ill temper showing on his heavy features. "She'll be back now, bringing all her mates no doubt. I said, what did you do that for?"

"She looked hungry." He had no fear of Chef who, in command of kitchen staff only, had no jurisdiction over William on the service side. He could take his annoyance to the *maitre d'hôtel* of course, but over one slice of bread? Which she hadn't taken, anyway.

Perhaps she'd come back. He hoped she would. He felt pleased with the tone he'd used to Mr Samson. Even so, he avoided the chef's eyes and hurried back to the serving dish to bear it off to the dining-room before Jameson, his station head waiter and immediate boss, noticed the length of his absence. No point courting trouble. In the eighteen months he had been

26

here, William had risen from humble clearer, *dibarras-seur*, to his present role. He'd come out of the army a corporal, unhurt if somewhat shaken by his eleven-month ordeal as a soldier fighting for a country that found no use for men who had risked life and limb for it. Luck, however, had singled him out immediately in the form of employment here at Letts, mainly, he surmised, because of his upright carriage – due to his aim to have become a sergeant had the war gone on any longer - and his suddenly discovered ability to ape the well-rounded tones of the better-class Londoner. All this to the joy and relief of his parents in Shoreditch who had feared for his well-being both in the war and, having come out of it unscathed, in civvy life too.

At Letts he had polished his adopted accent until it was no longer an effort. With it had come a sense of self-assurance, though it was never so imposing as to put up the backs of his superiors.

Letts was a high-class establishment with a fine reputation among the wealthy and the famous and a history harking back to the early part of the last century, he'd been told. Originally an oyster bar, it now served all kinds of expensive meals, mainly fish dishes, at prices humbler denizens of London could never hope to afford. This kept it exclusive to the dinner-jacket, top-hat and white-scarf brigade, the ladies in embroidered evening gowns, or at lunchtime in exquisite about-town Harrods suits or exclusively hand-made day dresses in fine Harvey Nichols materials. The restaurant consequently expecting its staff to measure up to such fine clientele, William ambitiously made sure he fitted those requirements.

Occasionally the place was visited by Mr James Lett, the old man getting on a bit now, and sometimes by the two sons, Geoffrey, who was the youngest, and Henry, who was a little younger than William, around twenty-one. Perhaps it was the age comparison that made him smile at William that first time, and perhaps he had liked William's returning smile, for not long after that, William found himself praised for his diligent work and told he'd be made up to a *commis*. He'd been a *commis* for five months now and had begun looking to go up one step further, but it seemed no further promotion was forthcoming no matter how hard he worked. Being cheeky to the *chef de cuisine* wouldn't help either.

Bending towards a diner and his lady in a gorgeous emerald evening dress with gems to match, Will deftly served the vegetables and reflected soberly on his attitude in the kitchen.

His thoughts drifted towards the pretty little waif to whom he had offered the half-eaten piece of bread.

Her eyes had been purest hazel edged with a darker shade to make them all the more startling. That was all he could remember of her – her eyes - and he hoped she would be back and that he would be there to confirm that that was the colour he had seen in that fraction of a second and that he was not just imagining it.

–

During the days that followed, he found himself waiting, hovering longer than he should when visiting the kitchen with his empty plates. He really had expected her to come back, as Mr Samson had predicted, maybe with a horde of gutter friends, but she didn't. Others came, were ordered away with threats of police, but she never returned.

Perhaps it was her very absence, but the more William thought of her the prettier she seemed to grow in his eyes. Common sense told him he was fantasising – she was just another grubby little gutter-snipe, probably, as people said, a scrounger looking for hand-outs without wanting to work in return. Yet she had said she would work, he remembered. And then his heart would swell towards the beautiful apparition his mind formed and he could not do his work as he should have.

Then, just over a week later, there she was. He happened to be in the kitchen. He saw Mr Samson notice her, raise his voice as it was ever raised without fail to his kitchen staff whether they did their work well or badly. And now he was making towards her with his ladle raised, still dripping soup.

"I warned you! Last time you was here I warned you. Come here once more, I said, and it's the cop-shop for you." It seemed the girl *had* been here again, then, in his absence.

Moving fast for a large and portly man, Mr Samson's free hand caught one of her thin wrists before she could turn and run. "Morris, fetch the police. There's always a copper on the corner of Jermyn Street. Quick about it, man!"

The young man flouring a tray of whitebait dropped the flour-shaker and scuttled past the straggling pair. The girl was making little high-pitched squeaks of panic, twisting the thin arm trapped in Chef's grip, her lightly built body wriggling frantically, the shawl she wore falling from her shoulders to reveal a holey cardigan, old cream blouse and shabby skirt. One foot in its patched boot kicked out but Samson evaded it easily.

"Oh no you don't, you vixen." With that he dragged her bodily into the kitchen – and bodily meant just that, she all but horizontal on the tiled floor and being dragged further from any source of escape. It looked as though her arm might be pulled clean out of its socket.

William sprang to her aid before he could realise what he was doing.

"Leave her alone! She's done no harm. We don't need the police."

He did not realise he had taken hold of Mr Samson's hand in order to prise it from a grip so fierce on such a thin wrist that it really must have been painful for the victim. When he did realise what he was doing, he let go immediately and stood back. This could cost him his job. It would surely be reported.

"Chef. I'm sorry."

Morris was already back, breathless. "I couldn't find a policeman anywhere, Chef. I'm very sorry, sir."

The girl, now quiet in his grip, was gazing upwards in the hope of being released. "Sir, I'm sorry. I won't come here again. I promise. I am sorry."

With apologies being repeated from all sides, the man looked from one speaker to the other. "Bugger me!" Samson breathed, his thick lips beginning to curl. "Being bloody apologised to from every direction. I like that."

His broad grin revealing large discoloured teeth, he threw a glance at those who had paused in their work to watch the fracas, but instead of shouting at them to mind their own business and get on with their work, he challenged each in turn. "Dodds? Potter? Whitelaw? The rest of you? Do any of you want to add to this apologising lark – *and make me a happy man*?"

There came a dutifully hurried chorus of: "Sorry Chef, sorry."

Samson broke into a sharp guffaw. "You should all be sacked, you lot." In a suddenly good frame of mind, he let go of the girl's wrist but caught her by the shoulder as she made to skitter gratefully away.

"Now, you, you've learnt your lesson I hope. Don't come back worrying us any more."

This time William stepped in with more assurance. "Chef, I'm sure she isn't a scrounger. I'm sure she'd work if you gave her a chance to. Can't you set her to cleaning the floors under the sinks and such?"

Samson looked at his little captive. "This one? I don't think so. She's heard what you've said, but I bet my last brass farthing the moment I let go she'll be off like a chased rabbit." William looked at the girl, again struck by the appeal in those eyes. They *were* hazel, a remarkable hazel, with flecks of green in them. "Will you?" he asked her. "Will you be off? Or would you work here, scrubbing floors?"

To his surprise, for he wasn't exactly expecting it, she nodded.

"I don't mind what I do. There just isn't any work for people like me. And all I want to do is support myself in the world, hold my head up."

She stopped there. Why had he expected her to add that she had to support a sick mother, an unemployed father, half a dozen younger brothers and sisters? It was the stuff of the silent screen – if the one-reelers weren't comedies, they were pathos like this.

"Do you just support yourself?" he found himself asking, and saw her nod. He would have loved to go into the question of why, but thought of duty and the fact that he had been out here too long; could be dragged over the coals when he got back into the restaurant by those at the table he was waiting upon as well as the somewhat jumped-up station head waiter, already seething with impatience.

He looked quickly, appealingly, at Mr Sampson who was still grinning his large-toothed grin, was still in his sudden but dangerously brief good mood and who now, to William's joy, gave the girl's shoulder a small shake.

"If I let go of you and say you can start with them tiles under the sinks, will you be away? If you do try to be away, you'll find I'm quicker than you and you'll be in my grip again and it *will* be the police station for you. Now then." He let go, his hand hovering over her. She stood perfectly still. "Right," he boomed, pointing to the fallen shawl. "Pick up your bits and come with me. I'll speak for you, but you keep your mouth shut."

Her champion, his over-long absence from his table preying weightily on his mind, hurried back with a small smile thrown at him by the girl to resume his duties and face the irritable frown of his superior.

–

The noise of pub drinkers punctured William Goodridge's thoughts and dragged him back to the smell of beer, the warmth of the pub, and to the young man opposite him. For a moment he had to struggle to recall the name. Edwin – Edwin Lett, the

33

young man who had voiced an uncertainty whether to sell his shares or not. The lad's brown eyes were on him, wide with interest. He must have been reminiscing far more than he'd intended. But now he couldn't recall quite what he had said and in what order.

"What was my father like, then?" Edwin was asking.

"Your father?" It was hard to focus his mind on the present.

"Geoffrey. When he was a young man. And my uncle, when he was young. What were they like?"

Yes, when the two brothers were young. Young men about town with not a care in the world, unlike the poor perishers struggling with no work, no means of support, no thanks for what they'd done fighting for their country.

Not that he held any grudge against the more fortunate, the more privileged. They were what they were and many a wealthy man's son had been slaughtered in the mud of no man's land alongside those who now struggled for a hand-out.

He had liked the two Lett brothers from the first. Fine fellows. A little reckless, but no side to them for all that Henry Lett had returned from the front – his brother had been too young to go – to the luxury of good living. They had both made the most of it, restive young men that they were, eager to have their fill of all the new experience this new life offered –

emancipated consenting young women, high living, responsibility thrown to the winds – and who could blame them?

Looking back it was almost natural to put oneself in their shoes, to know how they felt, to become one of them as they had been then.

Three

"A pretty girl is like a melody…" The song had embedded itself in his brain for three days now, like a splinter in the flesh refusing to be dislodged. "That haunts you night and day…"

All morning he'd been trying to pry it from his mind by thinking of something else to hum, but after a while, back it would come: "She will leave you and then come back again…"

Damn the thing! He and a group of friends had been singing it after leaving some night-club to go on to the Chelsea Arts Ball to see in the new year. It was 1920 now – an entirely new decade – the old clutter left behind with all the old sorrows of war and, so his girlfriends said, the restriction of corsets. He too was glad of *that* as he could fondle them more easily now. And there would be no more observing outdated rules of parents who for the most part were still stuck in the previous *century*, let alone the previous decade.

"A pretty girl is just like a pretty tune…" Damned silly song. The thing stuck in his head until it felt only decapitation would remove it. Defiantly, Henry hummed a snatch from *The Gondoliers* as he went down to lunch.

The gong in the entrance hall of Swift House having thrummed discreetly some five minutes ago, the house had fallen silent. After the glitter and noise of the Chelsea Arts Ball it felt even more lifeless than usual. Lingering in the past, it still lacked the grandeur and solemnity of a truly ancient and stately house. Swift House wasn't old in the sense that those ancient heritages were, having been built only a hundred years ago. Its first owner and builder had apparently served in the Indian Army and, unable to break with the romance of it, had designed the house in colonial style, even to the wooden veranda running the length of the ground floor and the set-back windows of the upper floor.

Impressive, but not possessing the ordered formality of older houses, Swift House was a rambling warren of passages, even the main staircase curving off one of them instead of dominating the main entrance hall to command all eyes to its stately flight as guests entered.

As a child he had loved racing along that maze of corridors, to the consternation of the staff, who were all certain that one day one of them would be tripped up and whatever they were carrying topple all over the floor. Now he viewed the place with distaste. Cold, characterless, charmless was how he saw it, with nothing of an ancient country seat that could hold its own in any age; sadly dated in the face of today's vibrant urgency. He felt ashamed to bring friends here whose own homes were mostly either full of three-hundred-year-old elegance or else starkly but satisfyingly modern with clean sophisticated lines and art deco simplicity.

Henry made his way down the stairs thinking again of New Year's Eve. It had been such a marvellous night, finishing off the year just perfectly. In fact his whole year had been pretty good. His father's business was thriving really well – contrary to the expected masses of unemployed following in the aftermath of the war, any who had employment had plenty of money to spend and they spent it innocently. He had come of age with lots of good times ahead of him, and so much more to look forward to: good times, great times, for people like him.

July had seen his twenty-first birthday; emancipation; and a huge party held in London at the Park Royal Hotel, a deal more fun than anything that could be held at his parents' home which, spacious and accommodating though it was, was far too isolated out there among the Essex flatlands of Halstead Green. They hadn't been keen on it being held in the heart of London. But twenty-one? They'd had to relent.

Of age at last to do as he pleased within reason, he'd spent the whole of September in Nice with a crowd of chaps and had fun with the girls there. It had struck him as strange: his last time in France had been with German shells whistling over his head, he ducking in terror as they burst with dull hollow explosions in the soft mud of once green fields, and offering prayers of gratitude at having survived each one. He had lived among clinging mud or choking dust depending on the time of year, rubbing shoulders with the dead and the wounded and the shell-shocked, and witnessing more blood than had been good for any twenty-year-old. To be whooping it up in Nice a year later with not a care in the world seemed odd indeed.

The Chelsea Arts Ball three days ago, again doing as he pleased. And what company! What sights! Girls half clothed! This being a new and enlightened age, freedom of spirit was in – in fact, the largest float there had held dozens of half-naked women, the statue it held totally naked and called the Spirit of Freedom. And dozens in fancy dress were as scantily clad as they could be: an endless parade of Roman ladies of the orgiastic sort; women of ancient Greece, Amazons, Red Indian and Stone Age maidens; Britannias and Boudiccas by the score, and of course the usual revealing art nouveau stuff, all the wearers with the same intent of baring thigh and as many other bits of flesh as they dared. The less adventurous, shielded behind medieval and Renaissance costumes or different shapes of Jacobean and Georgian crinolines, with a sprinkling of Queen

Victorias and Elizabeths dotted about, had cursed their cumbersome choices and eyed the freedom of others with envy.

Well after midnight, with the party still going strong, they and their dashing heroes, growing more drunk by the minute, had clambered on to the precarious floats until they collapsed into the tight milling press of party-goers amid screams of panic, delight and sheer exuberance.

Henry had gone as Charles II, his partner Mabel Thomhurst-Hill as Nell Gwyn, her nipples on show for all to see – very dark, plum-coloured nipples they were too – because, she said, in those days women did show their nipples and she wanted to be authentic.

She had added a black beauty patch to one of her pushed-up breasts and perhaps it was the beauty spot that did it, as it was in Restoration days no doubt designed to do, but it had all tormented him so much he could hardly bear himself and they had *done it* in a welter of lust for each other behind a Chinese screen in some below-stage dressing-room they'd found. It had been his first really joyful experience other than those with a couple of indifferent prostitutes he'd had while on furlough in Paris in early 1918 in a desperate attempt to forget what he would go back to afterwards at the front. That didn't count – this had. He'd imagined himself in love with Mabel as she squirmed and writhed and exclaimed, while he felt her bare legs wound around his waist, those full breasts of hers moving and pliable beneath his hands, his lips, the unexpected glorious warmth of her finally surrounding him.

Afterwards he had lost sight of Mabel in the tightly packed crowds and in the cold, barely grey light of New Year's Day had taken another girl home instead, one dressed as Joan of Arc, complete with chains at her wrists and sackcloth-covered bosom, only her Bible having been lost in the earlier melee.

Whether it had been her concern for the loss of the Bible – she kept saying it was her mother's and that she would get into such terrible trouble – or the chaste costume she was wearing – which was still in one piece, amazingly – he got nothing from her for his kindness in taking her home to her door. Still, he had been fulfilled by Mabel so he had nothing to be disappointed about. Henry hoped he would be able to see Mabel often. He had her address. He would look her up this afternoon after lunch.

Hurriedly he crossed the wide hall and entered the diningroom hoping he might not be the last to arrive. He was. Four pairs of eyes gazed at him from the long walnut dining-table as he entered – six, counting the parlour maid and Atkinson, their butler, though those two lowered their eyes quickly. As to the others, Geoffrey, nearly three years younger than he, looked amused, his sister Victoria disinterested, his father resigned, his mother... His mother was glaring at him, her eyes fiercely blue.

Smiling at them all and murmuring a perfunctory, "Sorry I'm a bit late," he took the empty place opposite Geoffrey. His father allowed a small nod of his head, occupied with splitting open a fresh bread roll with his two thumbs. His mother said nothing, but her face spoke volumes, compelling him to further his excuse.

"Bit of a headache." He heard Geoffrey titter. "Was having a lie-down, forgot the time."

"Heard the gong, though?"

Henry looked directly at his father, still preoccupied with his bread roll, buttering it liberally with a small round-ended knife as he spoke. It was best not to acknowledge the remark. Lately his father seemed forever preoccupied, lacking the vitality he'd once had. He seemed suddenly to have grown old. Henry sat back as the parlour maid came to stand beside him with the soup tureen, and nodded to her silent request.

"Henry." His mother broke the silence that had descended over the table, a silence that conveyed to him that he had been a subject of conversation prior to his making an appearance. "Isn't it about time you started taking more of an interest in your father's business? You *are* twenty-one now. You've had enough time frittering away your life by now."

Henry lifted his gaze from the tureen from which Susan was ladling soup on to his plate and, signalling her away, frowned over towards his mother in a rather whimsical way that held just a touch of annoyance.

43

"Mother…" When he and his mother agreed and all was well, he'd call her "Mater", playfully. When he was annoyed he called her "Mother". That should have been enough warning of his irritation. "I spent two years of my life *frittering* it away in the trenches."

"Other than that," she countered, matching his glare. "The war ended over a year ago. It needs to be forgotten, and you need to think a little more seriously about your future. One day the business will be yours. Yours and Geoffrey's. Geoffrey seems to understand that. Why can't you?"

Henry found himself wondering, as he listened to her speaking of Geoffrey as though he were not here, whether his brother minded that.

Didn't she realise that rather than being understanding, as she put it, Geoffrey was very good at making people believe he was; he was very good at pulling the wool over everyone's eyes, letting them think that he was quite adult, and all the time having too much fun to bother himself with inheriting his father's business. He'd told Henry as much himself, had been quite open about that.

"But as far as Mater is concerned, I'm the cherub of the family," he had grinned saucily before looking deeply into Henry's eyes, adding, "And you'd do well, dear brother, to emulate me, or you'll get yourself into too much hot water for your own good. Use your noodle, Henry. Keep your nose clean, as I do, even if you are having it off with every Tammy, Dilys and Hilary."

44

"I understand you haven't been near the place for weeks," his mother interrupted his reverie now. "How can you know how a restaurant is run if you don't show yourself? I gather you were out again all last night. Nor did we have one glimpse of you on New Year's Eve."

"I was at a party."

"Nor on New Year's Day. Only yesterday were we finally privileged to be allowed your company. You may have come of age, Henry, but you still owe this family a debt of respect. You treat this house as some kind of hotel and I won't have it. Where were you all day yesterday and all night too?"

All night in bed with Mabel. He was tempted to say it, but his mother must already guess where he'd been; she wasn't a cloistered nun. Having spent the morning of New Year's Day with a friend he had then gone to see Mabel. They had spent the day together, shopping, dining, going to the theatre. Then they'd gone to a hotel room together. And now he was madly in love with Mabel Thomhurst-Hill, totally and madly.

"It was too late to get all the way back here, so I stayed in London with some friends."

His mother's lack of reply was fraught with accusation. Pushing her plate away she remarked testily, "This soup is lukewarm." At which Atkinson signalled to the maid to take the plate away and, with the rest of the family having finished, remove theirs and commence serving the next courses, an assortment of cold meats and salad followed by cheese and

45

fruit. A light lunch, as Estelle Lett always preferred on Saturday, it was now being taken in silence, her disapproval of her eldest son lying like a blanket over them all, her thin frame in its pastel blue gown stiff and painfully upright.

As they made to leave the table for their various afternoon pursuits, she took her eldest son aside, her tone very quiet as she said, "Henry, I wish a word with you, please. In the drawing-room."

Following her across the hall deferentially, for the word "please" had held a note of domination, he stood while she seated herself in her favourite armchair, placed where the sun could touch her somewhat pallid cheeks. From there she looked up at him, her features stem.

"On Monday, Henry, you go with your father to the restaurant. There you will begin to apply yourself properly to the running of the business."

"Can't Geoffrey go?" he ventured.

"I want you to go, Henry," came the reply. "Your brother is three years your junior. At eighteen he is too young yet to be expected to settle himself down in order to learn the smooth running of the place."

"It runs pretty smoothly on its own," Henry said sourly.

"It runs smoothly because the wheels are oiled by your father's own hand. It does not run itself as you seem to imagine. The administration would go to blazes without your father behind it. It is he who presides over everything, who keeps the place running without problems."

"I thought that was the restaurant manager's job."

He was being very bold, but his mother's expression did not alter.

"And do you know the restaurant manager's name? No, of course you don't. Nor that of the *chef de cuisine.* Nor any the waiters. Nor the office staff. Your father knows the name of even the lowliest temporary kitchen hand. And that is what you are going to do – to know everyone by name, who they are, how they work, if they are efficient or lazy. That is what your father knows and that is what you will have to learn before you can ever dream of taking over the restauraunt when your father is no longer able. As I said at table, you have frittered away your days for long enough. You and Geoffrey are your father's heirs, and your father is not getting any younger. Henry…"

As she broke off suddenly, the stiff posture began to crumple, almost as if her frame was collapsing. Henry saw her eyes begin to glisten and her lips to work. Becoming aware that he had noticed the change in her composure, her back instantly stiffened again. One blue-veined hand lifted to indicate the sofa opposite her.

"Henry, sit down. I have to tell you something, and I need you to be sitting in order for me to tell you."

Mystified, he moved to comply, this being not an order as were most of her demands, but a request.

"Henry," she said again as he sat. "I shall have to tell you this before long. Geoffrey doesn't know yet, but he will have to be told, too. Your father is not a well man. In fact he has... he has not long to..."

The normally self-assured voice faltered. Realising that something was very wrong, Henry found himself automatically leaning forward to take hold of her hands. They were icy cold, and he now noticed that they were screwed into fists, the outline of the knuckles gleaming colourlessly through the tight skin. She let his hands lie on hers and seemed to take strength from the firm comfort of his touch.

"Your father has been to see his doctor. He has been having some amount of pain in his throat for quite a while and lately he has been experiencing difficulty in talking for any length of time."

Yes, he had noticed that his father said little to him – or anyone – of late, where once he had been a great teller of tales, of the old days, of the people he had met in his life, the tricks he and old friends had got up to in his youth and the events of the times. Henry felt he knew Letts as if he had lived those times himself; had often been forced to stifle a bored yawn while his father repeated himself with such enthusiasm that his stentorian voice filled a room as though his audience were at the opposite end of it.

The new taciturn man of the last few months had left Henry imagining himself in his father's bad books for his casual love of life and refusal to apply his mind to its more serious aspects. Now hearing what his mother was saying, he was sobered.

"Dr Griffith recommended your father see a Harley Street specialist. It was found your father has advanced cancer of the throat and nothing can be done. The specialist gives him a year, maybe less."

Her words had come out in a flood as if she wished to be rid of them forever and never be compelled to mention them again. In turn Henry could find nothing to say. The shock of what he had heard seemed to paralyse his whole body, his voice, his thoughts, his vision, every part of him.

From some way off he became aware that his mother was speaking again, her voice softer and gentler than it had been heard since he was a child. Yet it remained firm.

"The pain will get worse. He has pills to help dull it. But we have a terrible year ahead of us. We must do all we can for him, to lighten his suffering. And you must consider that perhaps by next year the business will have passed to you and Geoffrey. As the eldest son the responsibility falls on your shoulders. Geoffrey is very young, and he will need your guidance. So you, my dear, will have to learn to settle down and put your mind to leaving your carefree life behind you. It comes to us all, I am afraid. We have to learn that life is not a bed of sweet roses. It can be very harsh and very exacting and, at times, very cruel."

Well, he knew that. He'd been in the trenches. He had grown up then. But since then he'd been determined to make light of life for as long as he could. Having fought and seen death, he felt he deserved no less – and now had come this, to be told his father was dying and he must grow up.

Well, yes, he agreed with her. It was daunting, but he would shoulder the responsibility his mother was handing him, for two reasons; so that his father would never have cause to be disappointed in him, and so that he might convince his younger brother that life wasn't all fun and games and that he needed to knuckle down and help. Where the restaurant had once needed only one mature, level-headed man to run it, in the future it would probably need two of his and Geoffrey's calibre, not yet blooded in the hard-headed world of business.

Sitting very still, he saw his mother heave a deep sigh. "In any case, first we must take care of your father. The drugs will not give him all the ease he will need over the coming months. I will pray he does not suffer too much and for too long. I don't want to be without him but I shall pray I lose him quickly."

Listening, Henry felt his own eyes mist over. Unable to speak for the emotion, the varying pressure of his hand on hers speaking for him, it took a while to find his voice, and then it came hoarse with grief.

"I'll do whatever you want, Mother." There was only sadness this time in his address of her. "I promise. And you mustn't…" Whatever else had been on his lips he himself was not sure of, and he let it trail away.

There were no words. There could only be deeds now.

Thus Henry Lett began taking over the reins of the business, moving from a world of pleasure into one more formidable even than the trenches, where his fear had been basic, tangible, an animal fear, fleeting and forgotten in times of respite. This would prove to be amorphous and lasting, like his father's cancer itself, eating into the mind night and day, refusing to be got rid of. At times he didn't think he'd ever be able to cope. But cope he did over the next months.

Slowly he began to get to know Letts, the staff, from the most exhorted to the most humble, as his father had. He came to know young William Goodridge who, around Christmas, had caused a ruckus about wanting some skivvy employed; had gone to his father directly just before Christmas, improperly, over the heads of his superiors, to plead for a permanent job, just a menial one, for the destitute young girl on whom he'd taken pity.

The *chef de cuisine*, Mr Samson – he now knew his name – had been beside himself with rage, embarrassed by Henry's father's refusal to employ her. The sight of her rags had prompted a no to Samson, only for him to say yes a little later to William Goodridge, a mere *commis de rang*.

It seemed the man had made a practical nuisance of himself, but his boldness on behalf of a less fortunate creature, rather than earning him the sack, had touched the old man's heart. Very odd, that, for in his time Henry's father had been a hard-headed businessman, like *his* father before him. It was how the business had thrived. To relent as he had over some nameless ragged urchin was against the nature of the man Henry knew as his father. It could only be his illness that had made him so soft-hearted. The girl had stayed. Henry learned her name was Mary Owen.

The story of Goodridge's selfless audacity pricked his curiosity so that he made a point of making the man's acquaintance, much to the scowls of Ketteridge, the *maitre d'hôtel*, who saw his standing in this establishment as being somewhat insulted. Perhaps he was right. One did not consort with the lesser employees except to acknowledge a "good morning, sir" with a tight little answering smile of authority.

While speaking to William Goodridge put more than a few backs up, including his father's, it sparked off a surge of fellow feeling, as Henry asked him about the episode of the ragamuffin. It also allowed him to see those who worked there in a different light than his father had always done. These people were human, not just names. In no time at all Goodridge had him laughing at the near free-for-all in the kitchen during the Mary Owen episode.

Henry did feel, however, that Goodridge's pity for the girl had probably been misguided. Once she had herself enough money she'd be off spending it on drink or whatever, and her poor champion would feel dreadful having risked his own job for some thankless hussy.

–

Samson had been furious. "You don't go over people's heads. All right, Mr Lett has taken her on due to your interference, but you mark my words, lad, it won't serve you no good in my books. From now on you watch yourself."

William had said nothing, but the gratitude that shone in the eyes of Mary Owen, still working solidly and industriously weeks after Christmas and New Year had come and gone, did his heart good. He was prepared to be bad in anyone's books – in the books of the king himself, for that matter – for one smile from Mary Owen.

"You're getting on well," he told her. "Perhaps if you work hard, in time you might be given a better job."

"There aren't any better jobs for girls, not in places like this. Places like this don't have women cooking and being waitresses. Those jobs are only for men."

He had no argument for that. Women had shown their worth in so many ways during the war, taking on the jobs men had left behind to go and fight: had become clippies on the buses, even driven them, and ambulances too. They had taken up more presti-gious office work than they had ever been allowed to do before the war. They had trodden in the footsteps of absentee postmen, had come into their own at last as skilled workers in factories where once they had been thought fit only for mindless, menial tasks. There were even lady newspaper reporters now, young women training to be doctors and lawyers. Women over thirty were now allowed to vote, yet he had to admit there was still a hard core of jobs closed to women, jealously guarded by men.

"You never know," he said sagaciously, and hurried off to his own duties to escape the – was it adoring? – look in those hazel eyes, because if it was adoring it had suddenly embarrassed him somewhat.

It was hard to get her out of his mind. It worried him that she worked long and hard. Contrary to Chef's opinion that she wouldn't last a week – and to prove it, he had loaded all he could on her – March saw her still scrubbing floors, at other times bent over heavy iron pots and pans that Fred Dodds appeared now to have been let off doing by Chef himself.

William would watch her elbows, not quite so thin and sharp as they had been now that she had a little money to feed herself properly, going up and down like pistons, and his heart would go out to her. He would study her expression, taut with weariness as she worked, her small light frame hardly seeming up to the job – yet it apparently was, for she hardly ever let up to rest, and his own muscles would ache in sympathy.

Another seemed to be having feelings towards her, he noticed. Fred Dodds, these days doing the lighter tasks of removing used pots, scraping food off plates, stacking them for washing and putting them away after drying, ogled her constantly, promoting a strange sense of discomfort in William's mind.

Ten weeks after she had started, Dodds, with one eye trained on Chef, who was otherwise engaged, took the moment to sidle up to her, his tone a hoarse whisper that, hopefully, Chef would not hear. "Fancy comin' art wiv us ternight, Mary?"

She shook her head, continuing to scour the inside of a large iron pan with scouring powder and wire wool. "I'm too tired after all this. All I want to do is go home."

"Don't yer ever go art wiv blokes?"

"Never had time. Too busy trying to make ends meet."

"It's time you 'ad a bit of fun. Yer mum an' dad'll let yer art fer one night, surely. Maybe I'll see yer after work."

She didn't answer, and after work grabbed her threadbare coat from its hook in the single toilet she was forced to share with the male staff and made off into the darkness of the Saturday night before he could catch her. Seeing Dodds's bewildered frustration, William felt a thrill of what felt like triumph run through him. If he had any say in the matter it would be Dodds's last invitation to take her out.

The following Monday it was he who managed to get near her as she dried her chapped arms on a scrap of towel before beginning again on a new batch of grease-caked pans.

Taking his courage in both hands, he said casually, and quickly, because Chef would have no one loitering in his kitchen who wasn't working there: "Do you ever have any leisure time to yourself after work?"

Mary nodded. "Sometimes."

William took a deep breath, one eye on Chef coming through the long kitchen aisle in their direction. "Would you let me take you to the pictures?"

To his surprise and joy she nodded, but Chef, coming towards them, his ponderous gait displaying belligerence, allowed no time to make any sort of arrangement to meet.

His duties finished – early, thank goodness, with Monday seeing very few customers – he waited outside the restaurant for hers to be completed. Aware that his chance might dwindle before hardly having presented itself, he was looking to take her out this very evening but it seemed that the time for going to the pictures was growing less and less.

Finally she emerged, pulling her thin coat around her against the cold March wind. She looked surprised to see him. "You've been waiting here? You must be frozen."

It had been blowing steadily all day and now it was dark, he really was chilly with all that standing around.

"You said I could take you to the pictures?" he reminded. It would be a relief after this cold to be in the warmth and darkness of a picture palace. It would have to be the cheap front seats. He didn't have enough for dearer ones, paying for two.

"You didn't say tonight." She looked down at her threadbare coat. "I'd have to go home and change into something better. Wouldn't it be too late by then? I thought you meant another night."

"I hoped it would be tonight. It's not too late." He felt happiness drain from him at the thought of losing her company to another day, or worse, perhaps never to another day. "I could meet you somewhere."

She looked just as fearful of disappointment. His heart rose. It rose again as she brightened. "Come to my home while I change."

"What about your parents? What'll they say, a chap hanging around your door?"

For a moment she looked crestfallen. "My parents died when I was little." She looked only little now, standing there, her coat pulled around her slight frame. Her eyes glancing briefly away, she looked a child. "I live with an old aunt. She can't do much. Sleeps most of the time. I look after her, make sure she eats, that she's warm, that sort of thing. I don't have to keep her, luckily – she lives off a tiny annuity though it's hardly enough to support her at times."

She looked back up at him and the child was gone, her face momentarily reflecting the harsh life of those who had to struggle with it. Moments later she'd become young again, the indefatigability of youth winning through. "Come on, we'll have to hurry."

–

As she let herself out of one of a short row of tall old houses where she lived, an odd little street – almost an alley – tucked away behind the grand façade of far more imposing roads, the once clean brick-work fuliginous with age and years of London smoke, his first impulse was to buy her a nice blouse and skirt at some time or another should he be allowed to know her better. Nothing too expensive because that would embarrass her. Something modest off a second-hand stall, come by casually. In time he'd get her this and that, from better places, so that she'd look more presentable.

Not that he was ashamed of her, he thought hastily. How could he even consider it? Suddenly he wanted to buy her everything. His mind's eye saw her in a crystal-beaded evening gown, her fair hair, clean and shiny as it was since working at Letts, beautifully coiffured – at the moment it was drawn back into a loose bun – her lips ever so lightly rouged, her cheeks faintly powdered pink, a touch of mascara around her eyes. He saw long pendant ear-rings swinging, caressing her neck, the swanlike neck he knew to be under that old scarf she wore; a silvery bandeau around her forehead instead of that floppy old hat she was wearing; in her hand a…

With self-mocking, William put such thoughts aside – that sort of attire was miles beyond his pocket. Coming down to earth he crooked his arm gallantly for her to put her hand through it, and led her away to the bright lights of Oxford Street and a modestly priced, not quite so grand picture palace just off it.

Late, they arrived almost at the end of the first short film – a comedy with the Keystone Cops. But it didn't matter – they would see it round again and he was sitting here with Mary Owen beside him, her small face trained on the flickering silent figures of the grippingly dramatic Mary Pickford film, her eyes wide as though she had never seen a film in her whole life before while her mouth chewed unconsciously on the toffees he'd bought her.

From time to time he glanced at her, the glare of the screen lighting up her features, and he knew he wanted to be the one to offer a new world to her. It came to him as a shock, as he envisaged her in the splendour he himself couldn't afford, that he was in love with Mary Owen.

Four

Half of London's couples seemed to be strolling in Hyde Park this Sunday. The warm April afternoon had suddenly brought them out *en masse*, like the pink and white blossoms on the trees. At times it even meant side-stepping several in making their way along the park's criss-cross of paths. "And I thought we'd be on our own here," Mary giggled. She had her arm through his, he wanting more to transfer his to around her waist, though in the past when he'd attempted to do so she'd go taut with a sharp, "Enough of that, Will. We're in public," so that he'd take his arm away smartly, fearing to offend and lose her respect.

She held to somewhat old-fashioned standards – at least, he hoped they were merely old fashioned and not that she saw him in a different light to how he saw her, despite having gone out with him regularly these past six weeks. But with so many of the old morals and social behaviour thrown over in this new age by men home from the war with a new concept of themselves, and women who'd taken over men's places in the workplace throwing away all the old strait-laced attitudes, it seemed inappropriate for her to stick to stuffy convention.

It was the same with their goodnight kisses. Should his lips attempt anything firmer than a peck, his reward would be, "That's enough, Will." There was always an authoritative ring to her tone that belied her outward frail stature. At times he was proud of her strength of character, at others he was left worrying that she didn't feel the love for him that he felt for her. Yet she seemed willing enough to go out with him.

What worried him was the way she attracted the eyes of other men, quite unconsciously. Dodds, for instance, still ogled her.

"I noticed Dodds giving you the eye yesterday," he complained as they walked, the warm tang of newly cut grass, the first of the year, filling their nostrils.

Mary giggled again. "I think he still fancies me."

He didn't laugh. "You don't... fancy him?"

She stopped and looked at him, obviously insulted. "Good Lord, no! I wouldn't put up with that coarse creature. I hope you don't lump me in with the likes of that. I've been brought up differently. My Aunt Maud wasn't always old and frail. She was once a lady's maid and it gave her very high standards, and she brought me up to have values. You don't have to be rich to have values."

"No, of course not." She tucked her arm back through his and they resumed their strolling, the moment forgotten as she began to tug enthusiastically on his arm.

"Let's go for a row on the Serpentine, Will, then afterwards we can go and watch the riders along Rotten Row. I love the way they look down on all the spectators – think themselves so high and mighty. They're a scream really, don't you think? Putting on airs, and they're no different to us except that they've got money. Come on, Will, let's get a boat out."

Mary had a commanding way about her and he generally found himself conforming to her rules without question, which rather startled him at times. Again he wondered if she felt anything for him beyond friendly affection. She seemed happy to be here with him, yet after six weeks their relationship was still in its infant stage.

If only, he thought, as in his shirt-sleeves he pulled on the oars, she didn't captivate other men so, turning their heads. She was doing it now, albeit unconsciously, as she sat back at one end of the rowboat, hazel eyes boldly surveying all and sundry without realising the magnetism she possessed. But then, she was so pretty, her small figure in an iris-blue print dress she had made herself, its petal sleeves fluttering in the warm breeze about her bare arms as he rowed, that it was natural all eyes should turn to her.

It was the admirers closer to home that worried him. Apart from the ogling Dodds, whom he could dismiss, he noticed Mr James Lett's two sons in particular. Her head could so easily be turned by their open interest and by the money they had. Wouldn't any girl's?

It was indeed beginning to break his pocket keeping Mary's eyes on him; taking her to the pictures, even cheap seats provoked a need to count his small change like some miser. For theatre seats he was forced to line up, even for the gods, in all weathers, the queue stretching round to the dark and dingy rear of the theatre while the wealthy, alighting from carriages, went straight in through the wide and glittering main foyer doors, resplendent in impeccable evening clothes, all top hats and bow ties, their ladies beautiful to see even if without all the finery they might be the plainest women imaginable.

"Happy?" he asked her, and she smiled in reply, one hand delicately trailing in the water.

–

"Mother has been expressing quite a bit of surprise at your spending so much time in London with the business lately."

The statement was heavy with connotation that went straight into its goal. Henry threw his brother a glare from his armchair in the library. "I'm doing nothing more than she asked me to do. What's wrong with that?"

He was aware his challenge rang with deception, sure Geoffrey had defined it instantly as he shrugged.

"Just that she seemed surprised at all this sudden enthusiasm. Too sudden to be decent."

Henry closed his book with a dull slap. "Her words or yours?"

"Oh, mine, old boy. I merely wonder what the attraction is that keeps drawing you there."

Henry humphed. He knew exactly what Geoffrey was getting at. Geoffrey was as much smitten by that girl in the kitchen as he was. So were several others, all with the same thought in mind – "Who's the little beauty you've got working in your kitchen? She's a bit of a stunner, don't you think?"

One would think chaps wouldn't give a toss who worked behind the scenes of a restaurant so long as the food was top quality. Especially who worked in the kitchen. Especially a lowest-of-the-low kitchen hand.

He had made the mistake of showing one or two chaps around the premises now that his father could no longer go there, being too ill these days. They had spotted the girl immediately and, like crows descending upon a piece of choice meat, they had struck.

"Wouldn't mind a tumble or two with her. How've you kept your own hands off her so far? Or haven't you, you sly old fox?"

It wasn't like that. Mary Owen fascinated him – that was why he frequented the kitchen area more often than – as Geoffrey intimated - was decent. And yes, the thought had crossed his mind, but he had dismissed it. Firstly, it would be lowering himself to consort with a girl of his own staff, clean and neat as she was; secondly, she always looked so vulnerable, her smile shy when he appeared, that a certain need to protect came over him and the idea of seducing her as though she were there for his sole pleasure was unthinkable. Gone were the days when a master took his pleasure of a pretty employee. His father had done so, when he and Geoffrey had been small. It had caused a devil of a row between him and Mother when he'd been discovered. In those days wives of wealthy men often put up with such things, but Mother was made of sterner stuff and Father had received such a verbal thwacking he never went near a maid again, not as far as Henry knew.

But it didn't stop men being attracted to a girl like Mary, and he was certain Geoffrey would allow no scruples to mar his chances. The smooth-talking Geoffrey would have her as easy as kiss-your-hand; he was sure of it, given half the chance. And Mary? Being wined and dined and given a good time, with perhaps a little gratuity at the end of it, could work wonders with someone deprived all her life of such goodies. Geoffrey wouldn't stop at the once, either. Not until he finally got the girl pregnant, and then his interest in her would go out like a light being switched off.

Geoffrey was grinning. "Wouldn't be for some ulterior motive, would it, old chap?"

66

"I go there for Father's sake. We've all got to pull together, he so ill."

It wasn't a lie. Their father was desperately ill: on his feet and fighting every inch of the way, but in pain all the same.

Geoffrey grew instantly sad. "He's always been so strong. And now... I hate seeing him like this! And Mother's being so brave. But she's always been such a strong-minded woman."

His taunting forgotten, Geoffrey got up and hurried from the library. Henry suspected he needed to hide the sudden tears filming over his eyes, much as they were forming over his own. Their father couldn't have much longer. If God was at all merciful, he *shouldn't* be allowed much longer.

–

The middle of May on a Friday was the last time James Lett ever attempted to go to London, in the back of the Rolls, a rug over his knees. Feather, his chauffeur, was stony-faced these days, at a loss to recreate the general level of conversation that used to pass between them. Not that Mr Lett could speak any more except to croak a command, eyes front, and that seldom.

Henry sat beside his father, edgy from watching him as the car took its time. It tore him to see those cheek muscles so taut, contorting beneath the wasted flesh as every spasm of pain gripped the throat.

They didn't reach London. Half-way there, the already pallid face grew chalk-white, a hoarse gurgling that passed for a cough gripping the invalid. Obeying the waving hand to turn about, Feather swung the car round and speeded for home. James Lett was put to bed and the doctor called to examine him. It was the last time he left his house, though he was to linger for nearly another year.

-

William sat in the small parlour of the letting he shared with his parents, his sister married these past two years with a letting of her own.

The landlords called these properties "lettings", each floor having two or three. In fact the blocks of flats were termed dwellings by those who lived in them, each one comprising two bedrooms, living-room, tiny kitchen and small parlour. Every three or four years the landlords had them wallpapered and painted free of charge, and though poky, they were clean and presentable.

Not so where Mary lived. Her home was shabby, unattended to by whoever its landlord was, only a stone's throw from the dives and brothels of Soho – none of which, he was thankful to say, had rubbed off on her. It worried him to see the area in which she lived. It wasn't healthy. One day he hoped to take her away and give her a home here, in the so-called run-down East End where, at least in his area, most people lived cleanly.

It was the thought of his offer which loomed traumatic. So far he had not dared ask her to meet his parents. What if she said no, his suggestion tantamount to an invitation for them to start courting properly?

His father was eyeing him, faintly quizzical. "Looks like you're pretty serious about this young lady. She the same girl you've been going on about lately? Mary, you say?"

William nodded. This was the first time he had mentioned Mary by name.

"Mary what?"

"Owen."

Not that it should matter to his father. He returned his quizzical look, expecting to hear a deep guffaw break from the tall, lightly built man whose laugh one would expect from a far beefier man. It was not an infectious laugh, and was one which often embarrassed his listeners, who felt as though he had made fun of them.

Easygoing for all that, he made many friends and few enemies. He worked "in the print", as it was known, as a typesetter, earning pretty good wages in the bowels of the *News Chronicle*. William knew his father had hoped he would follow in his footsteps and that he saw the war as having initially stopped his son's career stone dead and afterwards afforded no immediate work for him. He had refused to see it was not just the newspaper unwilling to employ him, but that Will, with no desire to work in the dim electric light of a compositing room, would rather meet other people. They'd seen it, wanted no half-hearted workers when there were plenty willing to work their guts out.

Dad had been embarrassed by Will's going off to find employment of his own, as a waiter of all things. Effeminate, that was what he'd called it, even though William had always displayed a distinct liking for the girls, but he had slowly relaxed when William showed no sign of becoming odd, made happy at last by his declaration of wanting to bring this particular girl home.

"I am." William answered his father's first question. "Very serious."

"Have you told 'er?"

"Not yet."

"Then tell 'er."

"It's not that easy, Dad."

"Don't s'pose it ever was." He cast a wry grin at his wife, her once fair but now greying hair bent over her knitting. "Had a devil of a job getting round your mum in asking her to go steady with me."

She threw up her head, a smirk creasing her still relatively smooth features. "Come off it, George, you didn't do too bad. I weren't as awkward as that, was I?"

"You scared the life out of me."

"Made no bones about proposing, though, did you? Oh, I remember all right. Blunt as old 'arry, you were. What was it you said? 'What about it, then?' And I said, 'What about what?' And you said, 'Getting wed.' And I said, 'Yes, all right.' And you said, 'Right, then.' And that was it."

It was his turn to smirk. "Well, I'd got to know you by then."

"After blooming sixteen months, I should think you would have."

Listening to the easy banter – not always so amicable when Mum flew into one of her tantrums and Dad made himself scarce in double-quick time until finally the gale blew itself out in a welter of tears on his shoulder with him comforting her with a cuddle and patting her back like some old friend – it didn't seem it would be half so hard asking Mary to go steady with him as his dad had made out.

–

The restaurant closed, the last customer finally gone, all was quiet except for those clearing the tables, laying fresh white linen for the next day and setting out the gleaming cutlery. The lights low, the place quiet, they worked silently and swiftly, intent only on getting home.

Henry stood by the swing door leading to the kitchen, that area still noisy with the clash of the last of the pans being washed and put away. He had been there for several minutes before the young girl at the sink looked up to see him watching her. Immediately her face, already pink from the rising steam of the hot suds, flushed even deeper as she looked quickly away and applied herself even more energetically to her task.

Henry unfolded his arms and moved away from the door jamb against which he had been leaning, and as he came fully into the kitchen, his *chef de cuisine* looked at him suspiciously.

Mr Samson didn't care for having his domain invaded by the likes of Mr Lett's son, the "bloody young upstart". Henry had heard himself spoken of in this way to those working under Samson when he was not expected to be listening, the man daring his underlings to repeat it to anyone outside his kitchen under pain of death. Now Samson merely nodded with terse courtesy.

"Can I help you, Mr Lett?"

Henry shook his head but smiled graciously. "No, Chef, I'm fine. I thought I'd just come in to say that I thought you excelled yourself with this evening's food. It astonishes me how you manage with so few staff."

"Any more'd get under me feet. Too many cooks, they say."

"Yes, quite. Are you happy with the staff you have?"

"Well, sir—"

"I see the girl, Mary, is still working diligently. It was worth taking her on, I'd say, eh?"

"Matter of opinion, Mr Lett, I suppose. She could be worse, though—"

Henry had walked on past Samson mid-sentence, and had now centred his attention on the girl. "And how do you like your job, Mary?"

She had stopped working at his approach, her hands idle in the water, but she didn't appear cowed; rather she met his gaze with her own steady one, prompting a small twinge of admiration to explode somewhere deep inside him.

Her reply was equally forthright. "It's heavy going, sir, but I manage. I'm stronger than I look."

Indeed, for all her slight figure, Henry realised that it wasn't only her mind that was strong. She glowed with health, a far cry from the waif she had been on first coming here.

"I quite see you are. You appear to be wielding those hefty pots with such vigour." He realised he was flirting mildly with her. He hoped it didn't ring in his tone enough for Chef to detect, Chef with his jealous overlording of his little world, the last person he wanted to betray his present feelings to.

And he was having feelings. She was damned attractive. No girl that attractive deserved to be slaving at a sink under the harsh eye of the overbearing Samson. Henry could more easily see her in neat blouse and skirt, seated at a typewriting machine, books and papers about her. He could arrange for her to learn to type, maybe learn shorthand. Her eyes, when they had met his, were intelligent. She would learn office skills in no time at all.

Quite out of the blue he felt a need to see her in as comfortable a working life as possible. Again came that twinge of admiration – more than admiration – and now he knew why he'd been drawn to stand at the door to the kitchens to survey her; why he had more than once been tempted to do so, but had ignored the impulse with a grin of amusement at himself.

"Mary." His voice sounded strange. He kept his eyes averted from Chef, although the man was busy overseeing Dodds, who was taking out empty boxes and rubbish for collection in the morning by the dustmen. "Mary, are you any good at figures?"

She looked away now, applying herself again to her work. The pots clashed dully against the metal sink. "Figures, sir?" The wire wool scraped harshly against the iron rim of the pot. Henry found his gaze trained on what she was doing.

"Yes, adding and subtraction and multiplication."

"And division? I'm not bad at figures, though I didn't have much schooling. I left school at twelve." She hadn't eased up from her task. "My dad was killed in 1914, right at the start of the war. I had to leave school."

"Schooling doesn't matter. It's what you learn later in life that matters."

"You can say that again!"

He ignored the familiarity, the forthrightness that had crept in. Yet for some unaccountable reason it warmed him. "And your mother?"

"She died when I was eight." Her reply was monotonous.

This was getting away from his aim. He couldn't waste time on sentiment at this moment. "I've had a little thought, Mary. I would like to give you a little test to see how you can add and subtract and multiply, and also how you read. You *can* read, Mary?"

"Yes, sir. I go to the library a lot." She had slowed her sluicing of the pot, coming almost to a halt to look up at him again. Her eyes - lovely eyes they were, hazel, like amber with flecks of green in it - had grown questioning. "Why do you want to give me a test, sir?"

Henry found himself beaming. "Because if you are any good I might find employment for you on the office side of this business."

"Me?" Now she had stopped working altogether. And he was smiling idiotically at her, waiting for her response.

Chef had come back into the kitchen. He glared at his underling. He almost glared at Henry, a vague insinuation that this was not his employer's domain but his, and that the man was intruding, boss or no boss.

"You still wasting Mr Lett's time, girl?" he blasted her. "Get your work done and leave Mr Lett to his own business. I apologise, Mr Lett, for my worker's cheek. You, girl, say sorry to Mr Lett. We'll be finished in a tick or two, as soon as she gets a move on, and be out of your way."

Henry lifted a hand. "It's quite all right, Chef. I am in the way, I know. I'll leave you to your clearing-up. And thank you once again for the very good fare tonight. Not a single complaint. Not that there ever are, or very few. Not a thing out of place. We have a good staff here, Chef, kitchen and waiting staff alike. Well, goodnight to you." As he turned to go, his glanced at Mary. "Remember what I said, young lady."

Chef's pale eyes blazed. As Henry went out of the swing door he heard him blare: "What've you said to Mr Lett?" and her reply, "Nothing."

Leaving that night Henry hoped he hadn't got her into much trouble.

Five

Mary's face was radiant. "I can't believe my luck, Will. He came into the kitchen and, just like that, asked me if I wanted to work in the office."

Holding hands, they strolled through London Zoo in the May sunshine, past the throng absorbed in gazing at the fully grown male gorilla motionless behind his bars. His powerful bulk resting on the thick forearms which he had folded in front of him, his great black fingers clasped together, he gazed back at the chattering humans. His amber, bloodshot eyes conveyed – if the crowd cared to look closer, which they didn't – something like contempt, certainly curbed frustration, perhaps still remembering the misty freedom of some remote mountain lair, maybe even vaguely recollecting a group of chosen females and their infants, his offspring, which he had once defended with his supreme presence.

"I'm happy for you," William managed as he and Mary moved on past the gathering, the oohs and aahs fading behind them – but he did not feel happy for himself, nor content for her. Not only would he see less of her, but there was a question at the back of his mind as to why Henry Lett should behave so generously towards a mere skivvy in his restaurant kitchen.

He was conscious of prickles of jealousy running through him. Mary, cool in her summery cream cotton dress with its low waist, her fair hair recently cut in the shorter fashion so that its natural waves, released from its weight, now sprang lightly about her ears, was a pretty girl. More than pretty, she was striking. But for her petite figure she would have commanded rapt attention for she held her head high and her eyes steady whoever confronted her, even if it was the most important of her superiors. Chef didn't like her for it. He declared she lacked the humility dictated by her station in life and made a point of scolding her as often as he could. On several occasions he would have called for her to be sacked as a waste of the restaurant's money but for Henry Lett insisting that as a hard worker she warranted no such action.

That alone gave cause for jealousy in William's breast, for why should someone like Henry Lett go about championing the lowest worker in his father's employ if not because he was attracted to her looks?

"Mr Lett said he would get one of his office staff to learn me on the calculating machine," Mary was saying, now clutching his arm in her enthusiasm. "He gave me this test and found I was really good at sums. I knew I was, but it never stood me in much stead before and never seemed to matter."

"I shan't see so much of you – you up there in that grand place, and me still only a *commis* in the restaurant."

"We'll still be going out together. I'll see you then."

"You might lose interest in me, not seeing me so much."

"I'll never do that."

"There's three other men in that office."

Mary gave out a tinkling laugh. "Men! Two of them's married and the other's a boy of fourteen. I'm hardly likely to look at any of them, am I? There's another girl working up there, the one who's going to teach me to work the calculating machine, so I'll have company."

"I expect you'll see a lot more of Henry Lett, too," he said, the remark made to sound casual, its innuendo entirely lost on her.

"I expect I will," she said without hesitation.

They stood together in silence gazing at the lions in their square, foul-smelling cage, the concrete area bare but for one tree trunk scored white by bored claws, the cage bars so thick and close it was hard to see the pacing creatures in their full majesty.

William contemplated them for a while but his mind was more on the Lett brothers. They'd be rubbing shoulders with Mary every day, putting ideas into her head that she would never have had in her previous lowly state, making her feel that she was someone of importance, turning her head with their attentions. Who wouldn't feel jealous, his girl subjected to the interest of two wealthy and hand-some young men who could, if they wanted, give her all the things he couldn't? But he was being selfish. He should be glad for her. She deserved to get on. And she was still his girl.

Last week he'd taken her to see the ever popular *Chu Chin Chou* at His Majesty's Theatre. They'd had to line up for ages just to get into the gods, along with all the others who couldn't afford decent seats. But it had been worth all the lining up and jostling of elbows once they'd found a place up there. And Mary had been so taken by all the spectacle of the musical.

It had taken a great chunk out of his wages that week, though she seemed equally happy with less expensive pastimes, such as today's visit to the zoo. But at least he was making sure that she never lacked excitement. At the end of March he had taken her to watch the Boat Race. Cambridge had won and, both of them sporting rosettes in the light blue Cambridge colour, she had clung on to his arm as they stood on the bank of the Thames cheering the rowers onward and squealing with excitement.

That evening as he took her home they had kissed and cuddled in an alleyway. The way she'd returned his kisses confirmed that she was his girl and no one else's, and the possessive way she now clung on to his arm as they moved on past the lions' cage cemented that fact all the more, despite her new lofty position of assistant clerk.

"It's not a very grand post," she insisted. "I'm only a junior. I do all the mundane jobs, make tea for the office, run errands, do filing. I even have to clean the little cupboard where the tea's brewed."

But to him it was still a loftier job than being on the restaurant floor, though rather than feel jealous, he was determined to be proud of her. She'd go a long way. She had even vowed to rise to an even better position if she had anything to do with it.

–

"And how are you getting on, Miss Owen?"

Startled by the suddenness of the voice, Mary looked up from turning the handle of her adding machine to see Mr Geoffrey Lett standing at her elbow.

Colouring a little at his attention, she stammered, "Oh, I…" then collected herself. "I don't think I'm doing too badly. I hope I'm not proving a disappointment, Mr Lett."

"Not at all, Mary."

He was trying to sound authoritative but there were slits through which his youth beamed, making Mary smile; a smile he didn't see for she kept her face turned away from him as she affected deep concentration on the totals the machine was turning out under her hand. At nineteen he was hardly one year older than she and to hear him trying to assume the role of his father was amusing.

His father, James Lett, no longer came to the office. Mary had seen him once, when she had first started. He had looked ill and gaunt and terrifying, a man of disconcerting authority, one to make any new girl wilt and quake with fear. Had he been standing over her now, she knew she would have been reduced to that sort of behaviour, but Geoffrey hadn't the ability to make anyone quake. Wilt a little, but for entirely different reasons, her heart now pounding more rapidly at his unnecessary proximity to her.

"You and Mr Henry have done so much for me, giving me this job," she managed to burst out. She felt his hand lightly touch her shoulder and trembled briefly, just hoping he wouldn't notice.

It was June. She had been here six weeks now and was part of the office staff. From the very first day she had fitted in. Having cajoled William into helping her smooth away the last remaining rough edges of her English until she learned not to utter double negatives and mix up her tenses, she and the better-educated Edith Ramsey, who had been here a year and did the more coveted clerical jobs – certainly not the filing – got on like houses on fire.

"Not at all," Geoffrey Lett said in reply to her statement of gratitude and to her relief took his hand off her shoulder and walked off, back through the office door and downstairs to the restaurant from which appetising aromas were wafting, lunchtime fast approaching.

"They are both very nice to me," she told William that evening, as he seemed to want an almost daily report on her progress. "Both Mr Henry and Mr Geoffrey." But she didn't tell him of the reaction the younger Lett brother had provoked.

—

"Do you dance, Mary?"

"Dance?" The question took her by surprise. "Not that well, Mr Geoffrey." He was looking quizzically at her.

"I wonder, would you care to do me a great favour? You see, I've been let down. I've tickets for a Ladies' Night… You know what a Ladies' Night is, Mary?"

"No, sir." It often seemed a little ridiculous calling a young man a mere one year her senior "sir". But since he was her employer's son, she supposed she must.

He began explaining what a "Ladies' Night" was, to looks from those in the office: a narrow-eyed one from Edith Ramsey, no doubt jealous of the attention her friend was getting; indignant glares from the male staff who saw Mr Geoffrey as not conducting himself with enough decorum, conversing with such apparent familiarity with a mere office junior who'd not yet been here six months. Not that they could hear what he was saying; he was keeping his voice low.

"Have you heard of Freemasons, Mary? No? Well, I won't explain, but once a year the ladies are invited to what is known as Ladies' Night, a dinner dance given to honour the ladies who patiently allow their menfolk to go off without them once a week. My Lodge's Ladies' Night is always the last Friday night in October. That's only two days away and the problem for me is that one can hardly attend a Ladies' Night without a lady on one's arm. I regret to say the lady I was taking has the wretched 'flu. She'll never be recovered in time. So I wondered..." His voice had gone even softer, the rest of the office straining their ears, hopeful of catching a little of what was being said. "At such short notice I can't find anyone else. I wonder if you would care to go with me as my partner. No strings attached, I assure you. Just to be there with me."

Mary was stunned. Mr Geoffrey, asking for *her* company at a dance? Could he find no one else; a girl of his own class? Dumbfounded, she finally managed to stammer out as much.

"It's not every girl's cup of tea," he came back at her. "A bit tight-corset, so to speak. The girls I know prefer to let their hair down when we go out. I do desperately need to find someone to accompany me. I'd be most grateful if you'd agree."

He paused, and divining her reluctance, swept on hastily, "Obviously I don't expect you to have suitable clothes for such an occasion, so what I'd do to show gratitude would be to buy the necessities you'd need – the dress, shoes, handbag, evening gloves, and all else you'd need. And for your kindness in consenting, they shall remain yours, Mary. Yours to keep. Will you say yes?"

"Will it be posh?" With special clothes needed, of course it would be posh – beyond her simple capabilities.

"Yes, it will be rather."

"I've never been to a posh dance. I wouldn't know what to do, how to behave."

"It won't matter. I shall look after you. You won't be required to dance if you can't."

"Oh, I can dance." William had taught her quite a bit. He was a good dancer and easy to follow in the one-step and the foxtrot. He had shown her how to jazz, too, they going to a modest club, enjoying a glass or two of beer. Under his guidance she was doing well enough. But it wasn't just that, it was all the rest.

"I don't think I could sit and eat with the sort of people you know," she hedged, though she now wanted so much to go, for one evening to know what it was like to behave as though she were rich, rubbing shoulders with the well-off. At the same time it *was* asking a lot. She'd make a fool of herself. They'd point her out, laugh behind her back, or even to her face. Knowing her for what she was, they'd assume it didn't matter if they hurt her, this nobody. And what would she do if, so sure of himself, he left her alone for a moment? Like Cinderella she would run from the place, but, unlike in the fairy-tale, make a fool of herself. Yet his offer was an opportunity she'd never again have. She took a deep breath, teetering on the edge of desire. "You won't leave me on my own, not for a minute? I wouldn't know what to do."

"I wouldn't be such a cad. Not after the favour you're doing me." She was dumbfounded as he automatically concluded that she'd said yes to him. "Thank you, Mary. I know you'll enjoy yourself. I did forget to ask – you hadn't been planning on doing anything else on Friday, had you?"

"No," she burst out, suddenly excited. She never saw Will on Friday. Friday was usually reserved for washing her hair and soaking in the old tin bath her aunt kept out the back. Something told her that she should not tell him of Mr Geoffrey's offer. After all, it was only a favour to Mr Geoffrey and no point in causing a bother. William floated from her mind. She would have to make sure to wash her hair well in time for this dance.

–

James Lett's health had been declining rapidly since the summer until, with Christmas approaching, it seemed he might not survive very far past it, or if he did, much into 1921. It was heartbreaking to see him.

"I keep remembering my wedding day, when he gave me away," wept Maud, his eldest daughter, who spent more time at Swift House than in her own home these days. Her two children were with their nanny, her husband Gilbert quite able to exist at home with a decent staff at his elbow; she felt more needed here than there.

"He wept, poor Daddy," she recalled, weeping herself after visiting the sick-room yet again.

The house lay as hushed as if the sick man had already departed, Dr Griffith's portly figure going and coming with urgent regularity, his pony and trap – which in this day and age he still preferred to the motorised vehicle – becoming a common sight, while the nurse he had hired glided in and out of the sick-room with effortless silence as though on oiled wheels.

Victoria, standing at the foot of the stairs as Maud passed her, made no reply. Her eighteenth birthday was three months away. She was due to come out in the spring, and had been eagerly contemplating joining that long line of debutantes waiting to be presented to Their Majesties in the glittering blue-and-gold throne room of Buckingham Palace. She could see her father not now being there for this once-in-a-lifetime event in a girl's life, almost as glittering as her wedding day would be. It wouldn't be the same without him, without seeing how proud he'd be of her. It was this secondary loss, symbolic of the far more real fear of losing him, that made her weep quietly in tune with her older sister who had come out years before, enough years to have forgotten how it had felt.

Together they moved into the morning-room where their mother sat waiting for them before going upstairs alone to resume her sojourn at her husband's bedside. She was bearing it all with profound stoicism, if one discounted that betrayal of her grief in being there with him practically night and day until Dr Griffith finally had to order her to relinquish her vigil so that she too didn't fall ill just at the moment when she might be needed. She had taken his advice, but only briefly; when he wasn't there to see her, she crept out of bed in the dead of night to go and sit by her husband.

Henry was carrying on with the business as best he could, though he mostly left it in the hands of the head chef, the restaurant manager, and the staff they had under them, so that he could be with his father should anything happen suddenly. When he did present himself there, knowing that his supervision was needed in preparation for the busy Christmas season, it was obvious to all that his mind wasn't on the job.

Mary, throwing him sidelong glances during one of his rare appearances, felt terribly sorry for him, noting the constant gnawing of lips that twisted the otherwise strong young face, the light-coloured hair, with its tendency to curl, not as well groomed as it had been, and the grey eyes troubled. The man these days was never without a cigarette, and puffed with a sort of nervous tic, often lighting one as soon as the other had burned away as if being without one would set his mind thinking. A slightly built man, he had always expended much energy, but these days seemed over-full of it, again as though needing to block out thoughts.

As for Geoffrey – he'd asked her to drop the "mister" at the Ladies' Night to which he had taken her – she didn't know whether to feel sorry for him or not. He didn't appear half so affected by his father's state of health as his brother, spending rather too much time at the restaurant instead of at home when, in her mind, he'd have been better at his father's bedside while only one of them kept an eye on the business.

If anything even more handsome than his brother and slightly taller, Geoffrey had always blatantly concentrated his energy on himself rather than the business. These days he was here far more than ever yet contributed little towards the running of the place. His excuse, that he was needed, struck Mary as somewhat implausible. His brother did what was required. It didn't need both, the place already in capable hands, the head chef in sole management of catering and ordering, the restaurant manager in charge of the service side of things, neither warranting supervision.

Mary couldn't help wondering if she was the attraction, though she immediately reproved herself. He might have taken her to that Ladies' Night – which she hadn't particularly enjoyed, out of place amid all those fancy people – but that didn't give her leave to think herself something special in his eyes. She'd merely been a handy alternative when he'd been let down, the favour done, appreciation given in the outfit he'd let her keep. She'd not said a word to William about it all. Good job he didn't know. Hopefully he never would, the lovely things locked away in her chest of drawers. Yet the looks Geoffrey gave her left her wondering if this wasn't why he was here so often. But such suspicions had no real foundation and she chided herself for even thinking they had.

–

Her instincts were not so groundless as she imagined. Geoffrey's mind was definitely more on Mary Owen than on his father. He made the most of the opportunity to confide in her, often interrupting her while she worked.

"I don't know how I am going to shoulder all the responsibility of this place when my father is no longer here. I'm not even twenty-one yet. At that age a chap should still be having a decent time."

In this she did feel sorry for him. Then, when she thought of herself, she wasn't so sympathetic. From a very young age she'd had to cope alone. Her aunt, always a bit woolly in the head, was now becoming prematurely senile at fifty-four so that Mary had to fend for the two of them, and she now only nineteen. She had no time for people who couldn't or wouldn't shoulder up to responsibility. She even felt a stab of contempt for him beneath the fascination he still held for her.

"You should look on it as a challenge and face up to it," she told him bluntly, aware that the rest of the office was regarding them with a mixture of envy and disapproval – envy especially from the twenty-two-year-old Edith Ramsey, who'd confessed that she thought him an absolute dream, though she couldn't know that the boss's son and the humble Mary Owen had been out together, if only on a single occasion.

Her bluntness must have hit home, or else he too had become aware of eyes turned in their direction, for he nodded without speaking and walked away, his bearing very upright, leaving her regretting what she preferred to see as an obvious blunder on her part.

–

Mary Owen had accused him of not facing up to a challenge. Well, Mary Owen wasn't aware of it, but she was one of those challenges. A delightful little thing, but stubborn; since the Ladies' Night she had been unbearably formal, politely listening to what he said to her, as polite as she was with Henry. But he didn't want politeness. He wanted sighs and amorous looks from her. He wanted her to leap at his next offer to go out with him. But instinct told him he'd have to be prudent, making it appear as a small thank-you for the favour of her company at the Masonic do.

Nevertheless, it was weeks – just days before Christmas to be exact – before he plucked up courage to ask if he might convey those thanks by taking her to the theatre. Nothing grand (lest he overwhelm her again and frighten her off), just moderately priced seats to a modest show, a play or something. Did she like plays? Perhaps a pantomime would be was more to her taste. He hated pantos, considered them childish… well, they were for children, but *she* might like it. It was the price he was prepared to pay for a chance of her favours.

He caught her as she was leaving to go home, and, matching her own formality hastily explained that he wanted to thank her for all she had done in keeping him company at the Ladies' Night.

Her expression was one of amazement, the tawny eyes so clear they appeared to adopt a brittle, unwelcoming look. It was Saturday night. She was meeting Will outside. He'd be taking her home and then they were going to see the film everyone was raving about, Charlie Chaplin's first full-length film, *The Kid*. She'd heard it had made people cry as well as laugh and she was eagerly looking forward to it. The last thing she wanted was be late.

"You've already thanked me."

"I still don't feel it was adequate."

"You bought me a dress. I'd have thought that was enough."

"But I want to thank you just one more time. I'd like to ask if you'd care to let me take you to a theatre."

She gave a little frown. "When?"

"Tonight?"

"Oh, no, Mr… I mean Geoffrey. Not tonight."

He couldn't pretend he wasn't crestfallen, but his smile creased his face with assumed casualness. "What about next Saturday?"

"Not a Saturday. I go out with William Goodridge every Saturday."

At least it wasn't an outright refusal. He was encouraged. "One day in the week, then. How about a Friday?"

At the dance, made a little loose-tongued by all that wine, she had told him that on Fridays she always washed her hair and never saw Goodridge. That was why he'd plumped for it. She could wash her hair beforehand, as she had that last time. Despite having been a bit overwhelmed, she had enjoyed that night. He had been a perfect gentleman; had kissed her hand rather than her lips when returning her to that shabby little row of houses in Soho, all the time aching to kiss her lips, to touch her. If she consented to go out with him this time, he'd be bolder and get his kiss, maybe a little more. Having once gone out with him, she'd do so again, he was certain of it. He only needed to get her into the habit. She would soon forget this Goodridge chap who couldn't afford a fraction of what he could give her.

That evening at the Ladies' Night she hadn't stopped talking about this William Goodridge, a *commis de rang* in his father's restaurant who was apparently courting her, though, she'd mentioned, he hadn't yet proposed as such. Geoffrey vaguely recalled the tall, upright, good-looking man five years older than himself who waited at tables as though that was his sole joy in life, an expression on his lean face of utter dedication to his work; a young man with a prominent Adam's apple whose bearing and application indicated a promise of his going a long way in his career. One thing was for certain, on *commis* wages he could hardly possess two brass farthings to rub together for himself, much less provide any sort of future for a stunning girl like Mary. Yet she seemed full of him, where the two of them went – mostly places that didn't cost much, it sounded like, he saving hard eventually to have enough to ask for her hand. And good luck to him.

Not for a minute did Geoffrey contemplate stealing her from the man in order to make her *his* wife, for all she set his loins afire when he wondered what she'd be like in bed. Had he been married, she'd

94

have made a perfect mistress. As it was, he wasn't even courting; had celebrated his twentieth birthday earlier this month, was far too young to think of settling down although he knew of several girls who'd snap him up given half the chance. Time enough for that.

She was looking at him contemplatively, and, to his joy, asked, "What theatre?" She added, "I'd love to see *Chu Chin Chou* again. It was so lovely."

"Isn't once enough?" he asked. She shook her head vigorously, her eyes bright. Geoffrey sighed. So be it, then. Maybe he'd be rewarded for his pains. He hoped so. Mary Owen was more than a body could bear.

Perhaps afterwards they'd have an evening meal, somewhere quiet and secluded. Wiltons perhaps, where they could dine, just the two of them in one of its alcoves, and maybe he would hold her hand, speak about himself, his home life, his sick father, his already grieving mother, and, with her sympathy pricked, she would let him kiss her, gently, and then… who knew? He might be doomed to disappointment even then. Mary was proving a strong-minded person: not exactly prudish, but not easily fooled either. Still – nothing ventured, as they say. The challenge made him all the more eager to have her for himself. A challenge like that he could handle.

Six

Chill blasts of an early March downpour gusting in through the open door as a very damp porter hurried in and out with a delayed delivery of produce hardly pierced the heat of a kitchen preparing for midday lunches.

The head chef, having spent his morning going through the staff duty roster, upbraiding late arrivals, checking their excuses and solving maintenance problems, was now fretting at the delayed delivery of his order when he should have been checking the soups and sauces and the usual change of menu – one dish per section per day – as well as completing a hundred and one other tasks. He was not happy. It took a great deal of perseverence and patience to supervise a staff of thirty or more people. Samson possessed very little of either and by this time was a man on a short fuse.

This was how William found him as he crept through the kitchen on his illicit way back from the outside toilet. Pale eyes watched his approach, the man's arms akimbo, his chef's hat seeming to adopt an even more white and starched look at this intrusion, every vestige of the man affronted at his domain being used as a thoroughfare for the call of nature. To his mind the serving staff should be using the other, if chillier, damper way. He planted himself in the centre of the gangway, knowing this would oblige the offender to ease between him and one of the blazing coal-fired ovens to skirt round him.

"Hell's bloody name! Who said you could come through my kitchen?"

William came to a stop. "It's pouring with rain out there, Chef."

"Scared of a bit of wet, are we? Making this a bleeding habit, are we?"

It had only been the one occasion but William held his irritation at the unreasonable onslaught in check. After all, he was at fault, he supposed.

"Sorry, Chef," he muttered as he made to side-step the ill-tempered bulk. But as he came abreast of him, Samson's expression altered to one of unpleasant mischief which put William's back up, prompting retaliation. "It was an emergency, Chef. It won't happen again. I'm very sorry."

He had to raise his voice above the din of a kitchen in full swing, thus diminishing what little respect he should have conveyed.

Samson's heat-flushed fair cheeks darkened. Samson had no liking for him, William knew. Not since he'd handed that slice of bread to Mary the day she came begging for work without a by-your-leave, tantamount to laughing in the great man's face. Chef had neither liked it nor forgotten it.

"Sorry! Are you indeed?" Samson taunted.

Better not to argue. William made to move on around him but the man shot out a hand and grabbed his arm.

"As it happens I'm feeling a tiny bit sorry for you, young Goodridge."

It was a strange statement. William paused to look squarely at him, their eyes level, both men being tall, one slim, the other thick-set.

"Yes, I certainly am," Samson continued, grinning now. "You can't be all that overjoyed, the boss's youngest son taking a shine to your gel."

William became attentive, taut. "Who do you mean, Chef?"

"Now who else should I mean? The King of England? Didn't you know Geoffrey Lett had treated her to a little outing? Two, I gather, by all accounts. Seems he asked her to a Masonic do. Before Christmas that was. Then to a theatre as a little thank-you, so I hear. I mean, any gel would be flattered by attention like that. I'm surprised she didn't tell you!"

That last remark smacked of insinuation that he was being two-timed. "Where d'you hear all this?" Will demanded.

"Just what I heard." But Samson's continuing grin was saying, *That'll take him down a peg.*

"Well, you've heard wrong, or whoever you heard it from is a liar!" Shrugging free of the other's grip,

99

William sidestepped him and hurried on through the kitchen.

"Look to that gel she works with," Samson's voice followed him. "Envy makes for loose tongues. While you're about it, look to the heirs to the throne – the boys. Specially if she's not said a thing to you about it."

–

It seemed impossible that Samson's information had any weight to it as, with the March weather warming, he and Mary strolled along the Embankment that Sunday afternoon watching the different types of craft on the Thames, she clinging to his arm with a possessiveness that put the lie to everything the man had said.

She was chattering on blithely, and it was impossible to imagine her as any other than his girl. But he needed to broach the subject. Nevertheless, at the same time a voice in his head was advising him of the folly of asking outright. He could insult her. He could anger her. He could be told the truth and not know how to face it. Or be told an untruth and know it for a lie. He could lose her.

He didn't want to lose her so he remained silent. But his head seethed with conflicting thoughts. If what Samson had said was true, it was important she tell him of her own accord. But she hadn't so far.

If it was true, maybe it had been of no importance to her. Maybe she had merely obliged her employer's son by accepting his invitation to take her out on those two occasions. Reluctant to appear ungracious, she had probably seen it as a small token of thanks from him for all her work.

But what person forgets to mention a thing like that? Surely all that glitter and opulence must linger in her head. Mary was an ordinary girl from a poor background and would never take such an experience so much for granted that she could *forget* to talk about it. Why then keep it secret? And why the need to?

There followed an even worse fear. Did she harbour a secret fancy for Geoffrey Lett? It couldn't be mutual, a man of his standing. Maybe he was taking advantage of a sweet-natured, gullible girl. But Mary was not a gullible girl. Sweet-natured, but not gullible. Had Geoffrey Lett taken her out since and she wasn't telling?

The thought made him feel sick even as he and Mary walked arm in arm, talking with apparent ease. Here she was, commenting on women they passed: their clothes, their hats. She was giggling over snatches of conversation that floated by, remarking on the way the sun reflected off the river and how the river smelt so clean on a Sunday, so different to the rest of the week when it was busy with boats working and plying up and down. At this very minute she was saying how much she was enjoying being with him on a day like this. And all the time…

He smiled, patted her arm, looked down at her, knowing she had no inkling of the debate going on inside him. And when he finally took her home, after they'd wandered along Oxford Street and Regent Street and through Piccadilly Circus gazing into the lighted windows of all the large, expensive stores, she let him kiss her goodnight. But still he couldn't help thinking that she had probably been kissed by Geoffrey Lett, too. If she played her cards right with Geoffrey Lett, he thought bitterly as he kissed her, she could have all those things he could never give her.

The thoughts followed him home to plague him as he tried to sleep that night. And all Monday when he should have been concentrating on his work, they refused to go away. They wouldn't disperse until he'd had it out with her. But it wasn't easy to find the courage...

"Don't dawdle about it, man. Get that silver placed, now."

William came to himself and hurried to obey, but his station head waiter wasn't finished with him.

"Good God, man! You're like a wet weekend. That table there. It's half naked. It needs four settings and you've not even started on it. What's the matter with you, sonny? The customers'll be in any second. Well, get a move on!"

William began to dash about, instantly alert to all that needed doing, Mary thrust from his mind. He wouldn't be seeing her until Thursday. It was hard on the pocket trying to take a girl out every night and no girl cared to be incessantly walked along streets by way of entertainment. Though it didn't seem to worry Mary. Was it that she got her excitement from one better off than he?

For the next few hours he became the capable *commis*, serving the six covers on his station, bearing away the remains of meals. Ashtrays were emptied frequently, fresh ones supplied, extra cutlery brought as required, unwanted wine glasses conveyed away, crumbs appropriately cleared, tables relaid as customers left; silver flashing, fresh napkins were magically and skilfully folded, again clean ashtrays brought, wine glasses and cruets given a hasty last-minute glint. And all the time his mind was else-where.

He would tackle Mary about Geoffrey Lett on Thursday. It had to be brought into the open, if only to stem this heaviness that had settled in his chest.

"What's this?"

The question hissing in his ear, William looked up from brushing cigar ash from a vacated chair waiting to be occupied by the next customer's bottom on this busy Monday lunchtime. His station head waiter was holding aloft a gleaming goblet.

"There's a fingermark on this one!" he continued to hiss. "Get rid of it. Bring another. And jump to it then!"

William leapt to obey, all thoughts of Mary blasted from his mind for the moment.

James Lett lingered far longer than any would have expected. But now, after months of choking, fighting for breath, features contorted by the pain he had been required to endure, he went peacefully as a clear dawn arose after an April night of gusting wind and pelting rain. In the dim glow of a single bedside lamp, he seemed one minute to be breathing under the medically induced sleep Doctor Griffith had supplied. The next, without anyone being aware of the exact moment of death, he slipped mercifully away under the gaze of his wife, who had been with him the whole night, as she had every single night these many months until she looked as frail and drained as the dead face on the pillow which she continued to watch with a dry stare of disbelief.

"I think he's gone," she said simply.

Her two daughters, standing at the foot of the bed, burst into tears simultaneously, their gulps muffled by the closed curtains at the double windows. Her son, Henry, got up and very gently lifted the folded-back edge of the bedsheet to cover the face of his father, aware of the small gesture of protest his mother gave before letting her hand fall back on to her lap.

"It should be done," he whispered, almost as if the dead man could still hear him, but a ripple of guilt ran through him that his father bore an expression of tranquillity none of them had seen on this face in all these months; that it was near sacrilege to cover up this new peace on the stilled face after the twisted, pain-racked features that they had all become used to, though not inured to.

With the guilt came vague anger that his brother had not thought it important to be here on this night of all nights; anger that instantly faded as he remembered Geoffrey would not have been able to get home from Paris in time, even though the telegram they had sent would have reached him within half an hour of being sent. If only men could travel at the same speed as those electric messages.

Geoffrey had gone there for the weekend – to see a friend, he had said. He had left on Friday evening, would be back tonight, Sunday. True, no one could have envisaged Father going so suddenly after months of expecting it, yet it had to be this weekend of all weekends that Geoffrey had chosen to be away. With an unkind twist of anger against his brother, Henry wondered if Geoffrey would be as cut up about his father's death as he was, or stricken by guilt at being absent at the time of death. But such uncharitable thoughts were better brushed aside.

The dear face covered, he helped his mother to her feet. "We must send for Dr Griffith," he whispered and saw her nod in agreement. But almost immediately she sat herself down on a chair by the wall.

"I would prefer to stay here with your father a while longer, my dear, if you don't mind. He would not wish to be abandoned so soon. I will stay until he is well on his way. To wish him a safe journey."

Each word she spoke was emphasised by a small slow nod of her head as though she really did imagine her husband travelling some sort of lonely path, glancing reluctantly back but knowing he must continue; as if he would see her there waving him off much as she had waved him off when he set out for London in the limousine on Mondays and Fridays in the old days.

Henry nodded understandingly. She needed to be left alone with her husband, as she said, to see him on his way. She needed to be alone with her thoughts, her tears shed in private. That was Mother's way. Later she would emerge, head up, eyes dry, back straight, Victorian values intact.

With quiet unhurriedness, he ushered his two tearful sisters from the room. They were this century's children and felt no need to make any secret of grief.

—

For Mary it had been the most unbelievable thing. Having hardly come near her since last autumn when he'd taken her to the Masonic do and then the theatre, even presenting her with a proper dress for the former occasion – which he'd said she could keep and which now reposed in a drawer at home, probably never to be brought out again – Geoffrey had appeared to have forgotten her.

Christmas and New Year had come and gone, and with everyone so busy, it was understandable. But just as she had begun to resign herself to the fact that she had merely been a passing thing with Geoffrey Lett, best forgotten – and what did he want with the likes of her in any case when he had so many girls of his own sort to choose from? – he had come up to her in the office last month and casually asked if she'd ever seen the Oxford and Cambridge Boat Race.

Of course she had, last year, with William, but without quite knowing why, she'd shaken her head. And when he had offered to take her, it came to her that the last thing she wanted would be to upset Geoffrey's obviously well-meant offer by saying no. She had said yes, please, and his response, a bit alarmingly, had been to lean briefly over her to brush her hair with his lips and murmur, "Then I would be delighted to take you."

It was just as well everyone in the office had gone home. She had been just about to go too, the office dark and silent, though most probably he wouldn't have done it had anyone been there.

William had been obliged to work that Saturday – he often worked late on Saturdays, one of the busiest days of the week – and Mary had never found the courage to tell him of Geoffrey taking her to see the Boat Race. Instead she'd told herself over and over that there was no real need to, and as time went on the idea of Geoffrey asking her out again faded. She had squealed with excitement and jumped up and down as the race had drawn to a close and was sure she had so shown him up that he'd been glad to be done with her. As for her, despite enjoying the competition itself, she hadn't particularly felt at ease, a fish out of water among all those posh people. Geoffrey had remained gallant, however, had thanked her for her company and by way of thanks had taken her to a theatre in the afternoon. But it had merely been a way of disguising his disappointment in her, she was certain, and there had been no point stirring up trouble with William by telling him about anything, not even the fact that Geoffrey had kissed her – quite an ardent kiss really – before putting her in a taxi to take her home.

Then had come this astounding offer.

"Mary," he'd begun, again catching her as she was about to go home. Only the office manager was lingering behind, his office door closed though she had seen the man through the frosted glass engaged on the telephone, his back to her.

"I'm off to Paris this weekend," Geoffrey continued. "Was going with a friend to visit a mutual acquaintance of ours. We've bought the aeroplane tickets but now he can't go and I'm left with a spare air ticket."

"Air ticket?" She was already ahead of him, even as she dared not let herself believe that this could be an offer to go with him. Surely he wasn't expecting her to say yes?

"Daily air service between here and Paris was resumed last week," he explained. "It's an ideal opportunity to visit my friend. I don't suppose you've ever been abroad or up in an aeroplane, have you, Mary?"

It was an offer. It had to be. There came a sudden racing of her heart that he was giving her an opportunity that might never come her way again. Her voice had sounded small and weak.

"No, I haven't," she said and she saw him smile.

"What would you say if I asked you to go with me?"

"With you," she repeated idiotically. "To Paris?" When he nodded the only words she could find to say were, "I've got nothing to wear."

Her head had seethed with doubts. How would a place like Paris receive a girl like her? But his smile had broadened. "I'll buy all you need in Paris."

Her statement had been taken as a yes, but scepticism had plagued her right up to the time of leaving, that alone preventing her from saying anything to William. The whole idea seemed outrageous and improbable, even if she could have brought herself to hurt him – supposedly her beau - like that. She kept asking herself what girl would pass up such an invitation, kept telling herself that it didn't mean anything – she and Geoffrey came from different worlds, and all he was probably doing was getting a bit of pleasure in showing a girl from a poor background how the other half lived.

Trying to ignore a niggling guilt at having to make excuses to William for her absence, short though it would be, she said little to him, only that she was having to accompany her aunt on a visit to an old friend as she was not used to travelling as far as Southend on her own. "We'll have to stay overnight," she told him, "and come back on Sunday evening." After all, she had to be back at work on the Monday.

It was hard not to cringe at the lie, especially as William's expression was all-trusting as he said dolefully, "I know how you feel, love. Your trouble is you're too good-hearted. I'll miss you this weekend, but it'll soon pass." And again she had squirmed under the burden of her lie, actually wishing for a brief moment that she could wheedle her way out of this trip to Paris. But she had promised – and it was only one weekend, after all, and there might never be another chance. So she took heart and smiled at William.

"I'll be back before you know it," she said, and for the moment, that seemed to vindicate everything.

–

It was like a dream seeing England drop away as the aeroplane rose from the airfield with its sprinkling of flat, white buildings, the sight of a tablecloth of small fields below them strange to her eyes and presenting such an alarming drop that she clung to Geoffrey, who held her hand comfortingly.

The roar of the enclosed, single-engine aeroplane with its dozen or so passengers had been frightening at first, and she had been certain something was wrong with it, but before long she became accustomed to it, and the height too – a couple of thousand feet, Geoffrey told her grandly, though he wasn't really sure, himself.

Soon she was staring through the tiny window at the dully glittering ribbon of the English Channel, the boats resembling kiddies' toys. The undulating white coastline of France – looking like a huge map – filled her with wonder, with its vast fields, its tiny clusters of villages and towns. Paris finally came into sight and there were yet another scary few moments as the ground raced up to meet them, her stomach going over as they landed, the engine cutting off to leave her ears buzzing but the rest of her full of relief that they had come safely through this amazing ordeal.

Leaving the airfield, borne by taxi into the city itself, she gazed totally enraptured at the unfamiliar, busy Paris thoroughfares on this glorious sunny Saturday afternoon, incredulous that she, the owner of a brand new passport, had left rain behind in England only a few hours ago.

There was just one disappointing edge to it all: how wonderful it would have been to tell everyone back home about having winged across those vast miles in a couple of hours in an aeroplane; something few like her had ever done or ever would do. Yet she had to keep it a secret, especially from William. It almost turned the trip sour, but she shrugged it off bravely.

Alighting from the cab with Geoffrey's help, it was an intimidating experience entering the bright, carpeted foyer to be taken up to the room he had booked for her next to his, a lad carrying the two small bags for them.

Like her, Geoffrey had little with him. On his advice she had packed only a dress, a toothbrush, make-up, brush and comb and a nightie, he having said that all other toiletries would be supplied by the hotel, including towels. She didn't possess a dressing-gown, her outdoor coat sufficing in an emergency, though he'd said her room was an *en suite* one which, she found, meant having its own toilet and bathroom. Her home had no inside toilet, let alone a bathroom.

As they stood while the porter turned the key to her bedroom door, Geoffrey whispered to her that he'd changed his mind about seeing his friend. Looking at him and seeing him smiling, she let her gaze drop quickly. She was no fool. There never had been any *friend*. But far from feeling angry, she was flattered. Geoffrey Lett singling her out from all the girls he must know to accompany him here to Paris? It was flattering. But if he thought to get something out of it with her, he'd be disappointed, although a kiss or two wouldn't hurt…

The porter opened the door with a flourish and she found Geoffrey assisting her inside. The sight that met her took her breath and all other thoughts away but those regarding what she was seeing. "Golly! This all mine? I feel like a princess."

Geoffrey was tipping the porter who nodded and departed, closing the door behind him.

"You are a princess," Geoffrey murmured as she darted about the room which he'd said was only modest but which looked to her the most magnificent one she had ever seen.

"Come here, Mary." The tone of his voice, gentle but faintly masterful, brought to a halt her excited tour of the room and, questioningly, she went to him, to find herself surprised by his arms closing around her, drawing her to him. His face was bending over hers, his lips pressed down on her own before she had time to think.

It was as though an electric spark had plunged through her. For a moment she tensed. But she had expected this, hadn't she? Had been fully aware of why he had wanted to bring her here – not as a favour to him as that first time had been, nor as a gesture of goodwill, but for the same reason any man would ask a girl to share a weekend with him. She had consented with her eyes wide open and not even the rosy prospect of a trip to Paris could cloud her complicity.

The kiss had begun pulsing a strange excitement through her body, sweeping away the awe of being attractive to him, and, laying aside girlish pretensions, she willingly returned the kiss.

It was obvious what would happen. On the rose-flowered quilt she lay beneath him as he feverishly divested her of her skirt, her blouse. All the time his voice whispered in her ear that she was beautiful, that he loved her, had loved her from the first time he'd seen her, was unable to get her out of his mind, that he'd lived in torment of rejection, that he was utterly ecstatic that she felt the same about him as he did about her.

And she did. In those moments of climax, she did feel the same with a fierce pleasure that consumed and alarmed her in its unexpectedness. Never before having experienced such sensations, she even knew a moment of panic that it might cause her some unknown harm. But as he threw himself away from her to lie breathing heavily next to her, she stared up at the ornate ceiling, the feel of him still with her, and she knew all was well.

But then, gradually, misgivings began to creep into her head at what she had done, what she had allowed him to do. For her it had been the first time ever. For him… Mary felt her flesh chill. Not the first time for him?

She'd been so utterly stupid, had been totally carried away. But the urge to get up and put distance between them faded as quickly as it came, for it would have tarnished even more those moments of joy, as though she were no more than a woman of the streets. Instead she asked a question, harking on all he had said as he made love to her. "Geoffrey, do you really love me?"

Having said so in the throes of his passion, what if after all it had meant nothing, had been just words? Mary waited.

For a while he did not reply. Then he said slowly, in a low voice: "I never thought I'd love anyone like this."

It was all she needed. True joy overwhelming her, Mary leaned over him impulsively to lay a gentle kiss on his cheek.

"I love you too, Geoffrey," she returned, with confidence now, yet still hardly able to believe that she, out of all those he must have known, was his girl. She was still hardly able to believe that this was all happening to her. Her, ordinary Mary Owen.

But what about Will? All through that weekend, during which they made love repeatedly, the thought of how she was going to tell Will overrode the joy of knowing that henceforth her life would change. Geoffrey eventually proposing marriage would take her into the world of wealth and security.

Poor Will. Would he get over it? But there had never been anything binding in their relationship. He had only talked about marriage a couple of times, going on immediately to put obstacles in the way by saying that it took a lot of saving up for anyone to get married and it was more or less too early to think about things like that. No, nothing had been fixed, no engagement ring given. He had no claim on her.

Yet the thought of telling him all but spoiled the weekend for her, the most marvellous weekend any girl could want.

Seven

It was a sombre day, the day of James Lett's funeral, April shower clouds clumping together to make a flat and glowering mass by mid-morning. But despite the continuous light rain, the exceptional turn-out for the funeral was a talking point for weeks afterwards.

Every last one of his staff was required to be present, the restaurant closed as a mark of respect, the cost of some hundred employees getting to Halstead Green church paid by courtesy of his widow. Yet they were still only a third of the numbers who came. In life, James Lett had made a vast amount of friends and everyone who'd known him professionally or been in any way connected with him crammed into the tiny country church alongside the family. Lesser attendees were obliged to stand outside under a sea of umbrellas among the ancient leaning gravestones of those who had, perhaps more modestly, gone before him, their epitaphs for the most part indecipherable.

Mary and William had been found a place just inside the church itself, he expressing mystification as to why they should be so privileged compared to the rest of James Lett's staff. Standing with her head bowed as the coffin, borne on the shoulders of the pall-bearers, passed her with slow dignity to the low and solemn strains of a hymn, Mary knew exactly why they had been given this place.

Discreetly positioned at the rear so as not to attract too much attention from closer mourners or fellow colleagues, it appeared they'd merely been lucky to find space inside. Mary was just able to glimpse the back of Geoffrey's fair head as with his family he rose to his feet in the front pew. She leaned close to Will as every poignant note of the hymn, every measured step of the pall-bearers, prompted a twinge of guilt about standing beside the man who still thought her an honest, true friend and fiancee.

She had returned from Paris a thoughtful – and, in truth, downcast – girl. What had she thought she was doing, going off to spend the weekend with a man who surely had no lasting interest in her, for all he'd declared undying ardour every time they made love? Yet his passion had been so convincing, at the time she had believed every word. All the way home on the aeroplane he had taken such care of her, as though she were the most precious thing in his life. His parting words had been, "I must see you again soon, my sweet Mary." It had borne out his feelings for her. Then he had spoiled it by saying, "I've had an absolutely marvellous weekend."

Too lightly said. She had been merely the instrument of a marvellous weekend for him: now he could forget her, the insistence on seeing her again instantly losing all she had read into it, turning into a casual invitation. They could now go their separate ways until he fancied her again.

The last week had borne that out, it seemed. He had virtually ignored her. But then, his mind had been taken up with other things – guilt at not being present at his father's death, having been most likely making love to her at the moment of his father's demise. Such things would weigh on a person's mind. Indeed, she felt some of that guilt herself. Perhaps when things settled he might again turn his mind to her, but at the moment it seemed a forlorn hope. At least Will was constant. She should be satisfied, and she did love Will, really.

Will often wished he saw more of Mary, but his hours were long – he often worked from early morning until late evening, far longer than her office hours of eight thirty to six o'clock – and getting together was difficult.

His working day would run on until way past midnight if there was one of those late suppers with dancing afterwards for which Letts had become fashionable since the end of the war. "Let's go to Letts!" had become quite a byword with much of the smart set, the well-known and well-heeled descending upon the place after a theatre or night-club, the night ending only when the last stoic patrons had staggered off in the small hours. In fact Will had become used to famous faces: European royalty visiting London, even lesser members of England's royals, as well as stars of the London stage, the American stage, and now film stars. It all brought fame and prestige to the place, much as it had before the war when Edward VII as Prince of Wales had patronised it in James Lett's younger days.

Little thought was given to the weary staff who continued to smile and look as bright and sociable as when they had begun. Expected back at work next morning with only a few snatched hours of sleep, Will would bicycle all the way home to Shoreditch to let himself in quietly, his parents long since in bed.

The only good to come out of it for him were the high tips, if the supper-goers were happy enough, drunk enough and satisfied enough to be generous towards the staff who'd helped create the atmosphere which Letts bestowed with style. Geoffrey Lett's easy charm, wit and energy did much for the place, his brother rounding it off with his politeness, grace and friendly, easy-going nature. It all helped to please customers and bring out their small change.

For William, the smallest gratuity, saved religiously, meant one step nearer the day he could decently ask Mary to marry him. In fact customers seemed to take to him, often acknowledging the good-looking young waiter who worked hard and long, cheerfully and with friendliness, many referring to him by his first name. Having his station head waiter nod his satisfaction at him – good staff being a feather in his own cap – Will saw it only as means to an end; in time, maybe, he might be recommended for promotion and a resultant raise in salary. If only he had more time off to be with Mary, that was all.

He often worried that she must be bored during the time they didn't see each other. She had friends, of course, girls she'd known from childhood, and now and again a little crowd of them went to the pictures together, she told him, so she wasn't too bored. And last week she had gone with her aunt to see some old friend of the woman's in Southend, staying until the Sunday afternoon, which had let him off the hook, since he'd had to work late on the Saturday. She'd seemed tired when he met her on the Sunday evening, and of course she would be, having to travel all the way home from Southend with her aunt, who seemed to him to be quite a drag on Mary.

"You look a lot brighter than you did last week," he whispered as the coffin came to rest on the trestles before the altar rail and the congregation was asked to kneel in prayer for the soul of the deceased. "You looked so tired Sunday evening, I was worried for you, love. You do too much for other people."

He saw Mary incline her head, then bring her clasped hands up to hide her face. It wasn't a time to begin a conversation. He too bent his head as the priest began on prayers for the dead. He'd bring it up when this was over.

Letts was back to normal, once more thronged by parties of diners.

Henry was relieved. That first week following the funeral of his father had itself been almost funereal – quiet, as though his father's old clientele in some way felt they might be expected to adopt some sort of sentimental reverence, recalling in hushed tones the days of his strutting among them, laughing and joking; that not to do so might abuse his memory. Better to stay away than have what should have been a jolly evening ruined. They were, of course, sorry at the death of James Lett, but prolonged sorrow should not extend to them. It wasn't their business.

Moving between the many empty tables, the huge gilt-framed wall mirrors had reflected the vacant places, the painted ceiling and columns giving the whole a mausoleum-like quality where once they would seem to disappear amid the happy tumult of diners. The dance floor had been empty, the bar almost so, and Henry wondered if, with his father gone, the old crowds would ever bother to return. Perhaps they would find other, equally good restaurants – and there were plenty enough around the West End – preferable to the danger of constant reference to the sad demise of James Lett and the sort of embarrassment that can occur when one is unsure whether to mention a subject or avoid it altogether.

Time and time again Samson came out of his unusually quiet kitchen, his heavy jaw jutting sullenly as he complained of his staff falling into lax ways with so little to do, debating whether he should lay some off – something Henry could not contemplate. The sense of defeat if he allowed that, as well as the idea of compelling his staff to join the ever-lengthening dole queues 1921 was beginning to see, was unthinkable.

He had consulted Geoffrey about laying off staff. All his brother had done was shrug and voice an opinion that the place could be on a downward slope without their father there to boost it.

"He wasn't there to boost it for months while he was ill," was Henry's argument to that. "We kept it going. The place was always crowded. It can't make that much difference, Father being gone. We have to make it work."

Geoffrey's second shrug had angered him a little. Geoffrey showed so little interest in the place while eager enough to draw any profit – though for a while it had looked very much as though profits were a thing of the past and as though the place would finally have to be closed for lack of customers, wealthy customers. Henry shuddered at the thought of it even going downhill enough to end up as a lesser establishment to which workers came only at lunchtime, all its prestige gone, its name mentioned only with a pitying sneer – "Used to know it when it was filled to the doors with titled people, well-known people

– shame seeing it go like that." Such thoughts usually took the form of night fears – not exactly nightmares but the mind being left free in the small quiet hours to wander in chaos between sleep and lying awake, contemplating his father turning in his grave.

But over the second week came signs of encouragement: first a trickle of old faces among the casual customers, then by Friday the atmosphere beginning to liven up considerably. Now, three months later, Friday night was as seething as it had ever been with telephoned bookings flooding in daily.

Now Henry sidled between crowded tables, nodding to this famous face and the lady with him, to that titled host with his family about him, receiving nods of appreciation in return. "Doing a splendid job, Mr Lett. Splendid job."

Mr Lett – he might almost be his father. He looked like him, he knew. Maybe just a little of the good-looking part, but, judging from old stiff studio-type photos of his father, very much like him as a young man. Odd, though, that he should have Mother's ways, a tendency to be formal. He wished he could be more like Geoffrey who, while favouring Mother in looks, had inherited the easy, charming nature of their father.

Geoffrey should have been here tonight, but Geoffrey had a prior engagement – some young lady no doubt. Even so, as the other partner in this establishment it was his duty to forgo his amours and look to a little work, charming the customers as he was so good at doing – or at least being at home with Mother to allay her new lonely state.

"I say, good to see you, Mr Lett. Mr Henry Lett, isn't it?"

He turned to see a small party approaching, conducted to their table by the head waiter who was doing it with marvellous aplomb designed to flatter the clientele, exactly as James Lett had required. It was second nature to a gifted man such as Eustaquio Emmanuel, more usually known as Eustace.

The host of this particular party, whom Henry recognised as Lord John Felmore, a rotund little man, had detached himself from the rest of his party.

"I've been meaning to come before to extend my sympathies on the sad loss of your father – heartfelt, you know. Wonderful man. Wanted to be at the funeral but was abroad – couldn't get back in time. Still, never mind, better late than never, eh? So you've taken over. You'll be every bit as good as your father was, I've no doubt of that. No doubt at all."

Henry produced a sociable smile. He was good at sociable smiles, no matter how he felt inside, be it amusement towards a guest, contempt of his manners, personal despondency or, at this moment, this lingering grief. Yes, he could put on the charm – not the easy charm which came naturally to his brother, but he pleased his customers.

"It is good to see you again, Lord Felmore. I do hope you enjoy your meal."

"Oh, Felmore, please, Mr Lett. Your late father addressed me for years as Felmore. So now this is all yours, old man, yours and your brother's." His gaze transferred around the room and he frowned lightly. "By the way, where is your brother this evening?"

"Unable to be here this evening, I'm afraid."

"Pity. I like your brother. So jolly. Ah well, maybe we'll see him next time we come. But glad to see you fully in charge of… all this." He swept out a short arm to embrace the huge area of restaurant buzzing with life and filled with soft music until dancing began, when it would come even further to life. His action straining the button of his evening jacket, he chortled, "I take it you intend keeping the place exactly as it was in your father's day?"

"Naturally," Henry said quietly. "I wouldn't dream of anything else."

"Good. Best place in town. Best place to meet one's own sort. Pity your brother's not around. Where did you say he was?"

"Keeping our mother company. Early days, you know."

"Yes indeed. Early days."

The man had become instantly guarded – having already extended his sympathies, grief mustn't be allowed to go on too long and spoil his evening. "Must get back to the people," he said quickly.

Henry produced another warming smile. "If there is anything special you wish, do not hesitate to request it."

"Surely will. I take it the place stays open late tonight? A bit of dancing and a few extra larks?"

"For as long as you and your friends wish it, Felmore," Henry said, using the familiarity with studied deference, though not too much.

"Great, then. Great."

"I hope you enjoy your meal."

"Oh, we will, Mr Lett. Just like in the old days. Pity about your brother not being here. Still, never mind, eh? Doing his bit, being with his mother, eh?"

Henry continued to look pleasant. Inside, something was needling him. Far from considering their mother, Geoffrey was out enjoying himself, and Henry had a feeling he knew with whom. Gossip had trickled up from the kitchen – not widespread gossip, but from the mouth of the head chef in the form of a complaint that the little skivvy he had taken on was thinking herself too good for them all now, swanning around up there in the office, wearing dresses of the new and fashionable shorter length that a girl on her salary couldn't possibly afford, and that it was obvious who must be providing them, and a wonder that the young man she was supposed to be going steady with hadn't noticed the change in her.

Henry would never let what Samson had said go beyond his own lips, had cut his words short, dropping the hint – not exactly a warning, for no one *warned* the head chef about anything – not to let the gossip go any further for the good name of the establishment. He knew this sentiment would keep Samson, one of his most loyal and trusted men, tight-lipped from now on.

So Mary Owen was the girlfriend of one of his *commis de rangs*, William Goodridge. Then this suspicion – for that was all it was – of her larking about with Geoffrey should not be allowed to reach that man's ears. And if it was true, he felt mightly annoyed at his brother for playing fast and loose with some working girl. Mother would be appalled if she got to know it.

But it wasn't just his mother for whom he felt protective, it was the girl herself; a gullible young thing of… she could be no more than nineteen… taking the fancy of his brother who, young as he was, was no novice at securing a girl's favours, though she would usually be of better breeding. Somehow a need was provoked in Henry to protect her from herself.

Moments later, he was pulling himself up sharply in the unsettling awareness that there was more to this sense of protectiveness towards her than was good for his peace of mind. Sternly he hurried towards the front of the restaurant where he should be stationing himself to welcome in another large party of diners, two of whose faces the whole world recognised – the charming Douglas Fairbanks and the vivacious Mary Pickford, who had all eyes turning as they were conducted to their table. Henry immediately dismissed the twinge of apprehension he'd had thinking of pretty Mary Owen and contemplated on the immense prestige the arrival of this famed couple would bring to Letts.

–

What had been seen as post-war prosperity was collapsing rapidly due to a wordwide restriction of trade and an explosion in prices. Dole queues were beginning to consist not only of the unemployed war disabled but of those who had been in work, but who had been dismissed as employers themselves began to feel the hard times. Will Goodridge began to consider his own job, which until lately he'd thought of as secure.

A humble *commis de rang* still, it now seemed people like him were two a penny. If he didn't please the *maitre d'* he could be out this very day and someone more competent in his place – it was that easy to get staff, men willing to jump into any job to save their families from the struggle of living on eighteen shillings a week dole money bestowed on them for twenty-six weeks only. If he did get the push, then what would happen to his hopes of asking Mary to marry him?

There had been a moment of panic two months ago, with the business suddenly taking a plunge after James Lett died, that he'd be dismissed. But it had just as suddenly recovered. Even so, William still felt vulnerable. In the midst of the fervour that the two

Lett brothers, especially Henry, had displayed in their effort to return the restaurant to as near as it had been, if not better, he felt increasing pressure that, should he not meet the standard the new young owners had set, he'd indeed be out on his ear. But working even longer, harder hours, he was seeing even less of Mary, often having to be content with once a week, instead of twice as in the days when things had been a little easier.

Another concern was that lately she no longer seemed excited by the places he took her to, though he did his best to vary their outings together. In June they had been to see King George's official opening of the new Southwark Bridge. That should have been a novel enough outing, but apparently Mary hadn't thought so. They'd had to make an effort to see anything at all with people's heads in front of them blocking the view of His Majesty's entourage and crowds converging on the narrow limits of the new bridge. And though she didn't complain, the jollity in the air didn't seem to transfer itself to her.

Later that month His Majesty opened the Northern Ireland Parliament, but as they weren't there to see that, it didn't matter. But on the sixth of July came the official opening of the new King George V dock. Again William took her and on that occasion they had been lucky enough to glimpse the king shaking hands with workmen there.

"Queen Mary looks so small," Mary had remarked in surprise. "I'd have thought she was much bigger than that. The king doesn't look all that big either. I thought royalty would be taller. You expect it, don't you?"

"It's his beard, I suppose," William said. "It gives him a much larger, distinguished look." He was pleased to have been able to give her this treat, to see something of the splendid ceremony, if only the top half of His Majesty's head. She would never have seen the king but for him, and knowing that had done him a power of good. If only she had shown a bit more excitement. If he hadn't known her, he'd have said she'd been bored.

He thought of it now, abstractedly, as deftly and smoothly he served vegetables to Mr Douglas Fairbanks and Miss Mary Pickford, now Fairbanks's wife, and saw him lean towards her in an adoring manner. Both were unaware that their proximity to the waiter was almost stopping his breathing, even less aware that it was not who they were but what they did – gazing into each other's eyes – that conjured up thoughts that if Will's own Mary did not seem to gaze into his eyes very much, in truth she did love him.

He had come to learn that she could be naturally distant at times. Maybe on the day of the official opening of the King George V docks she'd been suffering from "that time of the month", though he wouldn't know for certain, so far not having had any intimate sort of relations with her even though they would kiss and he cuddle her until his whole being cried for more. He admired her strength of will, respected her for it, for at times she too must have craved for just a little more from him. After all, they had been going out together for nearly eighteen months now. All that time. Odd to think of it. Yet she could still hold herself back from any approach to making love. Yes, quite a girl was his Mary. How hurt she would be to know her good name had been besmirched by that toad Samson.

In all these months he had mentioned nothing of what Chef had said to him on that cold, blustery day in early March when he had trespassed into the man's kitchen to avoid going the longer way round to the outside toilet. It was an accusation no decent person would pass on to the girl in question, much less Mary who prided herself on staying unsullied until her wedding, as she had blushingly told him on a couple of occasions.

Slowly he had put it out of his mind, and if from time to time it still came to nag at him, he'd shrug it off. Mary was neither Geoffrey Lett's type nor class. She could have been – was as good as any duchess or debutante, could have knocked spots off any one of them. But he and Mary were ordinary people. Real debutantes and duchesses were way above them, so it didn't matter.

Eight

"What a dreadful thing." Mary's face puckered as William put away the *News Chronicle* dated twenty-fifth August after reading the account of the disaster with her. "Those poor people. How many was it?"

"Forty-four."

"Out of forty-nine. Just five of them survived. Oh, it's dreadful!"

"But if the airship had come down over the town instead of over the Humber it could have been far worse."

"It's still too many all in one go." She was thinking of Geoffrey at that moment, who had talked about sailing in an airship.

"I'd like to try an airship," he had said. "See what it's like to glide along a thousand feet over the sea. They say there's no sound when you're in one, not like aeroplanes. One day they'll be used all the time. Take you with me, eh?" He had cuddled her to him. "Maybe next year."

Speaking in terms of the future had made it seem so certain that he intended to share that future with her, for all he had not yet mentioned marriage to her, a fact which often set her wondering that she was becoming more his mistress than his intended. She didn't want that – didn't want this subterfuge, these secret rendezvous every now and again that were often too few and far between with he making love to her and she enjoying every second knowing that Will still saw her as unsullied, his girl.

So far she'd managed to keep the truth from him although the feeling of guilt hadn't got any less, and she dreaded the time when she would have to tell him. There were times, thinking of Will, that she wished the affair would die and she would never have to let on; others when all she wanted was to have Geoffrey ask her to marry him and the secrecy all be over. Yet somehow she knew that question would never arise. She was Geoffrey's mistress, whether she liked it or not. Men like him did not ask girls like her to marry them.

What did she think she was doing, allowing herself to be at the beck and call of someone like Geoffrey Lett, all stewed up when he didn't seem to need her and becoming all pent up when he did? She was a fool, a silly little fool. Knowing it, she shrank into Will's arms in a moment of despair.

"I do love you, Will. Couldn't we just get married?"

He gazed down at her with a small sorrowful frown, the newspaper in one hand forgotten. "I wish we could. But what on? I'm saving like crazy but it's not enough. I want to be able to offer you a proper marriage, but we couldn't live decently on what I earn. There'll only be the one wage coming in – you'll have to give up your job when you're married. It wouldn't be right, nor will they let you carry on office work as a married woman. And the way things are at the moment, I could be out of a job at any time. It's happening all over. We just couldn't manage."

"Other people do."

"Yes, hand to mouth. I don't want that for you, Mary. Let's wait a bit longer, till next year. Perhaps by then all this job uncertainty will blow over."

She had no argument, he seemed so adamant, but meanwhile the constant temptation offered by the wealthy Geoffrey Lett hovered, and she, silly fool, found herself quite unable to resist it, and hated herself for it.

These tears in her eyes, she told herself fiercely, were for the poor men who had perished in the R38 which had broken in two over the Humber and come down in flames. The whole nation had wept a little. But some of her tears, Mary hated to admit, were for herself, the mess she was getting into by letting herself be used by a man who was her employer.

Will's arm grew tighter about her, comforting away the misinterpreted emotion. "They weren't passengers on that airship. They were all technicians and crew. It was a test flight only."

"They still died, didn't they?" she said hotly and pulled angrily away from him, leaving him to apologise for his heartlessness.

–

Geoffrey had gone with his own friends to the South of France – fortunate Geoffrey. He hadn't invited her along: she wasn't good enough for his friends, Mary surmised and, shrugging off a feeling of inadequacy and insult, had turned to Will in the knowledge that her life lay with him, a solid future.

August Bank Holiday had seen her and Will going by charabanc to Southend despite the weather, huddling together under a raincoat in the open vehicle but, like everyone else, in high spirits. Will had used a little of his hard-earned savings to take her. He was doing his best.

"I know I'm supposed to be saving up for us to get married," he'd said. "But we do need the odd day or two off now and again." Pity it had rained.

Nevertheless, it had been a good day sitting under the promenade shelters on the Marine Parade side of the pier, which they had agreed was too exposed to walk along, watching holiday-makers scurry by and poking fun at the few hardy souls braving the wet to put their toes in the briny once the tide came back to cover the miles of Southend mud. Will's money had run to a plate of fish and chips eaten sitting at a table in a cafe, a cup of tea and an ice-cream, he saying it was time they ate in style. He had even made his cash stretch to a ticket inside the Kursall and they had taken a turn on one of the merry-go-rounds and the roller-coaster until Mary felt her fish and chips were in danger of coming up, that and the worsening rain putting paid to it all. But it had been fun, a small protest against a constant slim pocket.

To date she had enjoyed two other bits of excitement, both quite by accident and not costing a penny.

Firstly, one lunchtime, she and Will had been off at the same time and were having a wander towards Trafalgar Square to sit and watch the pigeons. They had found a huge crowd of protesters there, yelling and carrying on, demanding the release of nine councillors, newspapers having carried the scandal of their arrest for defying a court order to levy a rate on the people of Poplar who, though poor, already paid more than the average Londoner. It had been absorbing watching the police trying to soothe the crowd at the same time as arresting the noisiest and more truculent of the trouble-makers.

The second event had occurred two days after Geoffrey returned home. Again a crowd had formed, this one far pleasanter and only down the road in Piccadilly. Traffic had been held up as hundreds greeted the arrival of Charlie Chaplin at the Ritz. She and Will managed to creep out from work, along with several not directly in their immediate superior's eye, for a hasty gallop down the road – this once-in-a-lifetime spectacle not to be missed if it could be helped – and a hasty gallop back to work after a glimpse of the famous face without its battered bowler and the famous flashing smile without its comical moustache.

She and Will came together on the perimeter of the crowd. Trying to crane her neck over a sea of trilby hats, she squealed as Will lifted her with his hands around her waist so that she could see better. But Chaplin was prominent enough, having got up on the seat of his open-topped motor car to doff his hat and wave it at his public. Elegantly dressed in a grey suit, wavy hair immaculately groomed, the small trim figure was obviously delighted to see so many come to welcome him, appeared almost surprised by it.

"Isn't it exciting?" Mary was shrieking. "Ow... William, your hands are hurting my waist."

As excited as she, he let her back down to the ground gratefully, eager himself to get a better glimpse of the great man. Beside him, Mary was jumping up and down, cheering and waving a handkerchief she'd produced from the short sleeve of her dress. "Mr Chaplin! Oo-ooh! Charlie!"

She had become so overwrought that William's attention was taken from what was going on over the heads of the crowd.

"Isn't it just absolutely *wonderful?*" she was squealing. "Don't you think he's so *awfully* marvellous?"

The words she was using suddenly struck him as false – "awfully", "wonderful", "marvellous" – gushing words he had never heard her utter before. Not at all like the Mary he knew. He smiled, mystified by these new turns of phrase, this new Mary.

"He's only one man," he understated deliberately, his own excitement forgotten, but she wasn't listening.

"Charlie!" Her voice was carried away by the calling all around them. "Oh, Will, did you see? He looked at me. I think he saw me. Oh, darling, how divine! I'm sure he looked at me."

An odd, dull sensation of despondency had come to settle in William's breast. It wasn't just the mannerisms she was using, it was the way she was beginning to dress, the hems creeping up above her calves lately to reveal a little too much leg – fine for the overtly fashionable rich, but on her it didn't seem proper. And there was the way she was starting to act; almost as if she was aping them, those females on whom he waited, their conversation filling the restaurant with the self-same false, vastly overdone exclamations, where she had always had a mind of her own. Why? He was happy enough with her as she had been. He'd even told her that, but she'd laughed at him, asking why she shouldn't try to keep up with the new fashion of shorter skirts. He had wanted to tell her it didn't become her, but held back, not wanting to sound offensive. But he couldn't help wondering about this need to change.

"Fancy seeing him in the flesh," Mary was saying breathlessly as the great comic, with a final wave to the crowd, finally alighted from his motor to be ushered into the hotel. This was the Mary Owen whom Will knew, rather than one of the flighty young things she had been emulating only moments before. "I expect that's why we've had a rash of Charlie Chaplin films lately."

They had. Reruns of old films – *The Vagabond, The Immigrant* and *Easy Street*, all of which Will had taken her to see, since they didn't cost too much.

It was hard for Mary to come down to earth after all the excitement.

"To think," she continued to sigh, clinging to William's arm as the crowd started to disperse, though quite a few stalwarts still lingered on in hopes of another glimpse of their hero, perhaps from one of the hotel balconies. "To think – me seeing Charlie Chaplin in the flesh. I still can't believe it."

As she spoke, something made her look to her left, some force or other. The eyes that had taken her attention from the spectacle of Charlie Chaplin in the flesh, she saw now, belonged to Geoffrey. He was standing a little removed from the main throng, apparently watching her.

Instantly Mary's happiness fell away from her. Silent now, she gazed back, his eyes holding hers for a moment before he turned abruptly and moved off towards Letts.

"I don't think we ought to loiter about any more," Mary whispered, pulling at Will's arm. "We ought to be going back. Been away too long."

"Perhaps you're right," he agreed. "There's little else to see and we should both have been at our places."

Together they hurried down the side street towards the restaurant, leaving behind a still sizeable, hopeful crowd. In the distance a cheer went up, indicating that the film star had graciously come out on to his balcony. Too late to turn back now. And she no longer had heart for it anyway.

In the quietness outside Letts she parted company with Will, he saying, "See you Sunday," and she nodding absently, only half hearing him.

Of Geoffrey there was no sign.

–

"Seen much of him while I've been away?" Geoffrey whispered, the rest of the office having made for home, grateful that tomorrow, Saturday, was only a half-day, the rest of the weekend theirs.

He had hovered in a passage out of sight for some while until nearly all the office had gone, hoping Mary might not be in too much hurry to be first to leave. He couldn't know that she was deliberately lingering, certain that, after their exchange of glances, he would seek her out when the others had gone.

Until then he had made himself scarce, poring over the catering accounts with Samson; checking the stores – to Chef's suppressed annoyance, for there had been no need for checks; making the same nuisance of himself with his *maitre d'*; prolonging conversation with the lunch guests he recognised and who were mostly happy to chat with him and enjoy his fine repertoire of pithy jokes. All that in an effort to keep away from Mary's workplace.

Now he had come into the empty office to pose his question.

She moved awkwardly past him, going for her hat on its hook behind the door. "Who?" she asked inadequately. She knew who.

"That Goodridge chap you keep company with."

Gathering her hat from the peg, Mary gave a little smile with more embarrassment than warmth in it.

"Does he yet know about us?" he went on.

She hadn't put on her hat, was standing between him and the door, not moving, not looking at him. "I haven't told him."

"Is that because you feel something for him, or because you don't think I'm serious?"

"A bit of both, I suppose."

It sounded like defiance, a challenge. He needed to take up the gauntlet, know where he stood.

"Do you want to call it a day – you and I?"

"No!" The cry forced itself from her. Conveying exactly what he had wanted to know, it sent a surge of relief and joy through his breast. Going to her, he kissed her, briefly at first, but as the tingle which the kiss prompted in her brought her arms about his neck, he pressed his lips down on hers more urgently, the same feeling shooting through him.

While he had been away she had slipped out of his mind, but after a while, and as the days of fun and sun drew closer to their end, her face had come back and all he could think of was having her in his arms again. At times like that he was sure he was head over heels in love with Mary Owen, so different from the other girls who hung about with him, the wealthy, pampered, silly girls.

"I've missed you, Mary my darling," he whispered between kisses. His loins ached for her. "God, how I missed you."

"I missed you too, Geoffrey," he heard her whisper against his lips.

Tonight. He'd have to have her tonight. A hotel room somewhere…

A sound by the office door made them jump clear of each other. Both saw him at once. It was Geoffrey who found his voice first, Mary not daring to utter a word. With an effort, he made all appear casual, as though however he was caught and whoever he was caught with should make no odds. And it shouldn't. Henry knew him well enough not to be shocked.

"Henry? What're you doing in this neck of the woods?"

Henry's expression didn't change but beneath the bland contempt could be read something else, though what it was Geoffrey couldn't define. "I saw the office door open. I see now why it hadn't been locked. Who usually locks it? Mr… ?"

"I sometimes do, Mr Lett." Mary's voice sounded surprisingly efficient, if a little high and rapid. "The office manager often trusts me with the key."

"Yes, I gather you are doing well here." Henry's tone was one of quiet assertiveness. "Clever girl, Miss Owen." Geoffrey's ears, however, detected quite a different meaning to that appraisal, one which he understood straight away. "Well, lock up when you've finished, Miss Owen," Henry added evenly, his inference still acute. "Are you in tomorrow morning?"

"Yes," she answered, this time in a small, defeated voice, as though she too had detected the connotation to the words "Clever girl".

Geoffrey felt obliged to spring to her aid.

"See here, old man," he began, but Henry had already turned on his heel and was gone down the stairs.

–

It was unusual to see Henry in such a mood. He was normally a man who preferred to keep his feelings to himself, much as his father had done. To see him now pacing the morning-room, so full of passion, brought his brother up sharp, though he still saw no reason for all this "hoo-ha", as he liked to term any business that had an unnecessary ring to it.

He flung himself into one of the ample armchairs, the leather puffing up around his shoulders. "So you caught me at it, kissing the office girl. So what? Why all the hoo-ha about a kiss? You should know me, Henry – I usually do love 'em and leave 'em."

"Not on the premises you don't."

"Oh, come off it, old man!"

Geoffrey leaped up from his seat and went to a small occasional table that held a Lalique statue of a slim young dancer in a long, wide-skirted dress, a cigarette box, a table lighter and a crystal ashtray. Opening the box he extracted a cigarette, closed the lid with a sharp little click, stuck the cigarette in his mouth and flicked the heavy lighter, all with swift angry movements. Sucking in a lungful of smoke he blew it out with the same angry motion.

"What's so special about the premises?"

Henry turned his head towards him. "It's just not done, old man. If one of the staff had come back…"

"What if they had?"

"Well, what do you think? Think how would they have treated Miss Owen after seeing what you two were getting up to."

Geoffrey sucked in another lungful of smoke and blew it out in exactly the same manner as before. "Come on, Henry, we weren't having it off on the office floor, now were we? A kiss, for God's sake."

Henry had begun to pace the room. "If I hadn't turned up when I did, who knows, maybe you might have gone further."

"Huh! I could find better places than that to enjoy the favours of a girl. I know how to treat 'em. A nice dinner, champagne, flowers."

"I know that all right."

"And what's wrong with that?" Geoffrey challenged, riled enough to glare at him. "So you've got your mind more on business than enjoying a good time. But I prefer a good time. And I'm playing the field. I'm not pledged to any girl as far as I can see. At my age I'm not exactly looking to be tied down. Until I do, should it be any of your concern if I look for a little bit of pleasure? I do my share in the business and keep pleasure separate."

"It is when you start taking your pleasure with someone like—" Henry stopped himself abruptly, then went on, "With someone on our own doorstep." But Geoffrey had noted the sudden pause. He began to grin.

"What's the matter, Henry? Fancy our Miss Owen yourself, do you?" He saw a faint colour come into his brother's cheeks, noticed the lips tighten briefly. His grin began to widen. "That's it, isn't it, old man? You do fancy her. And you going all pious on me. Well, that's a turn up for the books."

He stubbed out the half-finished cigarette in the ashtray. "Who'd have believed it? Staid old Henry Lett with a fancy for a bit on the side with our own little office girl. You dark old dog!"

Henry moved over to square up to him. "You can cut that sort of talk out, Geoffrey. I feel nothing like that for Miss Owen. To me she's a damn good worker, and clever—"

"So you said when you came up on us, but I took it you meant something quite different. She knows where she's going, that one. And now she has both of us slavering after her. Can't go wrong, can she?"

Henry's open palm flashed out and caught his brother a smack on the cheek. Geoffrey's hand came up to touch the quickly smarting place, but then let his hand drop, the grin that had briefly left his lips returning.

"My, my! You do fancy her. I'm sorry you feel so strongly about it all, old boy, but I think she has her sights set on me rather than you."

"It's not the way you imagine." Henry had stepped back a pace, upset by his flash of rage. Now he turned his back on his brother. "I see her as a vulnerable young girl to be protected. She doesn't know the world enough."

"Oh, I think she does."

Henry ignored him, speaking as though to the window from which he was now looking out on to the grounds below, where his mother was talking to the gardener. "I'll tell you this, Geoffrey, if you lead her to believe all you tell her when none of it's true –

if you let her think you love her then cast her off and leave her stranded, I'll make sure you—"

"I do love her." Geoffrey felt himself gasp – not audibly, but his chest filled with the sharp intake of breath. His brother seemed no longer in the room. All he saw was Mary Owen. All he felt was this strange surge of love that had come and taken him so by surprise.

Nine

Only moments before seeing Henry Lett standing there, Mary had felt the familiar arousal flooding over her and knew Geoffrey had been aware of it too. But whatever might have come of it had been ruined. After the exchange of words, Geoffrey, with a hasty apology to her, had hurried after his brother, leaving her standing there alone.

Her tummy going over a little, she had listened to the raised voices in the passage below. Then the downstairs door to the restaurant slammed and she had stood in the silence, uncertain what to do. She had waited, but Geoffrey did not return. Finally, taking hold of her wits, she had gathered up her hat and dolly bag, and, locking the office door, dropped the key in among the lipstick, cream, powder, purse, comb, mirror and handkerchief, to follow in the wake of the two men, by then gone.

That they'd been arguing over her was obvious. That they found need to gave her no sense of achievement, merely confusion. The older brother's manner had been odd, to say the least. If he had merely disapproved of what he had come upon, his business premises being used as a seedy rendezvous – well, then, of course he was within his rights to upbraid her as an employee. But he had seemed more shocked at finding the man to be his brother. And it had been more than that, even – those hints, as though he had taken it all personally, that strange look on his face, one she still couldn't define or forget, so that after he had left with such noticeable abruptness, any further time she spent with Geoffrey would have made her feel cheap and tarnished.

She felt poorly equipped to deal with things like this. The moment had preyed on her mind and grown in strength as she made her way along the passage behind the restaurant to the muffled sound of diners, and into the twilit street. She was allowing herself to be dazzled by Geoffrey Lett: what he had said earlier in the year – "When we marry, maybe" – was still etched on her mind, the words perhaps not as genuine as she had believed, for all he had spoken them so earnestly at the time. He had never again mentioned the word "marry" and she'd not had courage enough to raise it, even now conscious of her status for all he'd taken her to Paris and had made love to her. She was beginning to realise that Geoffrey's word, like most everything about him, had to be taken with a pinch of salt; arrangements and promises alike were made without thinking – many had been the time he said he'd meet her only to tell her he wouldn't be able to keep the date, leaving her to wonder if some other girl hadn't turned his head for that evening. And their meetings were so few and far between; surely if he was in love with her he'd have made it a point to see her more often than he did?

All the way home these things had nagged at her. The world of Geoffrey Lett wasn't real – at least, for her it wasn't, more a dream, like peeking at something through a window, longing to be part of it but unable to touch. Worse, it was causing her to feel ashamed of her own life and where she lived. Not all at once and not, at first, obviously, but her feelings had begun coming out in little things she said, often some disparaging remark dismissing her aunt as a doddery old fool, a nuisance, a drag, when not all that long ago she had looked on her with kindness and affection and respect for what the woman had once been – a bright and efficient lady's maid – not what she was now.

Geoffrey Lett, she had concluded on reaching the dingy district where she lived, was better kept at arm's length. Better still, she would keep away from him altogether. It was as some of the old people said: if you get above yourself you often raise your nose so high you don't see the muck you're about to tread in – and muck sticks to rich and poor alike. Better to take heed of it and try to forget being discovered with her lover by his own brother. But the weeks had not lessened the shame. Neither did they diminish the memory of the wonderful weight of Geoffrey's naked body on hers, though she vowed to get her feet back on to firm ground and put the memories from her.

Even now, a month later, still traumatised by the event, she was giving him no opportunity to be alone with her. She made sure to be the first to leave at night, hurrying off through the last minutes of daylight at quarter to six, though the days were fast becoming shorter. Only once, two weeks ago, had she been delayed. Geoffrey, apparently having been awaiting his chance, cornered her. At the end of the day, the lights in the office – its few and tiny windows necessitated them being on winter and summer to help eyes see the work more efficiently – having been turned off, he approached her and started to speak, but a voice from the manager's office interrupted him. Making a hurried excuse, Geoffrey had moved on past her on the pretext of having a word with Mr Baines and she had slipped out.

For two more weeks Geoffrey stayed away from her and the office. Then suddenly, at three-thirty one afternoon, with everyone at their desks, Mary gasped, seeing him in the doorway, his fair handsome features full of animated excitement. But he wasn't looking at her.

"Listen, everyone," he began in that free and easy way he enjoyed with high and low alike. "I've had it passed to me that a very special person will be lunching here on Saturday. The booking has been made for a party of six, in the name of none other than…" he paused for effect, then went on with scarcely controlled emphasis "…the Prince of Wales."

A awed murmur went round the small office. Mr Baines gave a gentle cough to bring his small staff back to attentiveness, and Geoffrey continued.

"Now, if anyone happens to be in the office, occupied in doing a little overtime, shall we say, then I shall allow you down, one by one, for a peek at him. Just a peek. That's if you care to."

If they cared to? No amount of humphing and clearing of Mr Baines's throat could stop the buzz of excitement. Mr Geoffrey was a wonderful stick to allow them, his employees, this privilege. None paused to take note that Geoffrey himself was overrun with excitement, as was his brother, already talking to Samson about the special menu to be put on. The Prince of Wales's patronage would make the name of Letts known throughout London, just as it had been for many many years after the old King Edward had patronised the place when he was Prince of Wales, way back in 1892. The Great War and an entirely new set of people with new pleasures had obscured the memory, although Letts still treasured the crest *By Appointment of HM King Edward VII*. This new appointment would secure Letts's reputation yet again; they would reap bookings by the wealthy, the titled, heads of state, even foreign royalty, for years to come. Geoffrey looked at Mary, smiled, and left.

"I want you to come with me, Mary. Will you?"

Mary stared at Geoffrey, caught between not wanting to be lured again and wanting desperately to go with him, to attend a private little party thrown by the Prince of Wales himself in someone's luxury penthouse – dear God, not something to cast aside lightly.

Both Lett brothers had been included in the invitation to this intimate gathering, as a special thank-you for lunch and later dinner at their wonderful establishment. The Prince was reported to have remarked on its amazing decor, its dazzling setting, the warmth of its welcome, the politeness of its staff and the smooth efficiency of its service. "Better than anything in Paris," he was heard to remark with an easy, youthful, slightly high-pitched chuckle.

Mary had been granted her turn to peek at the smooth young features and was surprised how boyish he looked. To her eye he seemed unexpectedly vulnerable for a member of the royal family which she, like many, considered to be full of dignity and confident bearing that made whoever they turned their eyes upon immediately bow or affect an instant curtsy.

"He looks so young," she whispered to Geoffrey standing behind her as she peeked around a screen erected for the purpose of shielding the royal glance from the proletariat.

Geoffrey had taken her there after most others had taken their turn. Left until last, she began to suspect him of trying to punish her for avoidance of him. But now she knew why she had been left until last. As he stood behind her in that secluded space behind the screen, she felt his hand steal around her waist.

"He is young," he said, and the hand moved up underneath her blouse. "Young and handsome. Like me," he added with a hint of flippancy. "Has his fair share of female admirers and makes best use of them. *Not* like me. There's only one female I care for." His tone, low already, became even lower. "That's you, Mary."

At his touch, her first instinct had been to draw away from him, but she hadn't. And now her body leaned against his almost of its own volition.

"Henry has cried off from this evening," he crooned, his hand still cupping her breast, sending shivers of delight through her. "Mother isn't too well, still grieving the loss of our father, and Henry felt he needed to be with her rather than living it up with royalty."

This last had a sarcastic ring to it to which Mary's only response was a small twitch of a smile. That was what she liked about him, that light approach to most things in life, even though he too must have felt his father's going acutely.

"So, I have to go alone," he continued in the same crooning voice. "Unless you come along with me."

"Me?" The word wrenched itself from her, and she was sure it had been heard clear across the restaurant above the discreet tinkle of cutlery. Though no one looked up, she repeated the query more softly.

"You," Geoffrey whispered, his face leaning forward so that his cheek touched hers. "I want you to go with me. I am allowed to take a lady guest."

Mary's breathing threatened to choke her. Her heart began thumping against her ribs with sickening blows. She did indeed suddenly feel sick. "I couldn't. I couldn't face... royalty. I wouldn't know what to say."

"You don't have to say anything. I doubt if he'll even expect you to curtsy. This is supposed to be an informal little do before he goes off to India – his first proper formal royal engagement. He says he needs to be with friends and unwind. It seems his parents have no idea about his giving an informal party. They prefer him to be surrounded by equerries and all sorts of official people when he mixes with ordinary people like us."

Mary felt her lips twitch again as Geoffrey referred to them both as ordinary. At this moment she felt anything but ordinary – scared stiff, but not ordinary. Geoffrey, himself far from ordinary, was actually inviting her to accompany him to a *tête-à-tête* party being given by the Prince of Wales. Women fell over themselves to dance on the same floor as he, to be breathing the same air; to actually touch him or be spoken to by him went beyond their wildest dreams. And here she was about to share the same small private penthouse room with him, maybe be asked to shake his hand, have him smile at her, speak to her. She felt faint – sick and faint.

"Oh, Geoffrey…" He thought this much of her, to want her to be with him on this unbelievable occasion tonight. "I… I've nothing to wear."

"Wear the dress I bought you."

"But I can't—" she began in confusion.

"I want you to come with me, Mary," he said now. "Will you?"

Suddenly everything was all right. "Yes," she said.

–

The party was intimate: eight people in all, including her and Geoffrey. Edward, as he asked to be called, was accompanied by a young woman he referred to as Lady Charlotte, who looked so debonair that Mary was awed by them both, and would have stayed in a corner out of it all had Geoffrey not held her arm most of the time. He understood her feeling a fish out of water, despite the lovely evening dress he'd bought her in Paris, shimmering calf-length citron-yellow with narrow straps that showed off her shoulders to perfection. When anyone spoke to her, she found herself stammering, putting on an unnatural accent, trying to keep a hot blush under control as she smiled and replied – rather like that first time at the Masonic do. But an hour of champagne cocktails, the smoke-filled atmosphere and the unbridled manner of the three other woman dimmed her inhibitions and before long she too became witty, laughing easily at others' wit, Edward himself remarking on her tinkling laugh as quite captivating which made her grow hot again and avoid too much free laughter lest its "tinkling" jarred in the Prince's ear.

He and his companion left around one in the morning, having been present for a little less than an hour and a half. The rest continued for at least another hour, quietly talking and drinking. With Prince Edward gone, it all became a little boring, people discussing things of which she had no expert knowledge. Slightly stupefied by cocktails she decided that she must educate her brain, so becoming more like them, though it seemed they were talking a lot of twaddle most of the time. She was becoming concerned about her aunt, too. Though she had told her she would be late home and her aunt would have gone to bed quite happily – the old lady was capable enough to see to herself and quite unaware of time so that she would sleep like a log, in the morning treating Mary as though she had been there the whole night – she had felt a nagging sense that she should really be home with her by this time. If her aunt had by chance become worried, aware she was alone, she had only to knock on the wall and their neighbour,

Mrs Trench, a kindly chatterbox of a woman with no husband to nag her, would have come in to sit with Aunt Maud until she decided to fall asleep. She had a key, loved doing things for the old lady and with a tendency to insomnia would sometimes chatter on until the small hours, liking nothing better. She had given an eye to Aunt Maud that weekend Mary had been in Paris. Her aunt would be all right, and fretting seemed unnecessary. Yet fret she did.

"I'm going to have to go home before long," she had said prior to Prince Edward's departure, but with Geoffrey insisting it was still early and champagne cocktails dulling her concern, she had stayed on.

Now, with everyone gone, their host – whose name she couldn't recall, along with all the others apart from Edward and his Lady Charlotte – having offered to have them stay overnight, she lay beside Geoffrey in the sumptuous second bedroom of the penthouse, still a little giddy but her heady laughter long since ended as she and Geoffrey made love.

She remembered their making love. Less well did she remember their host offering them his spare bedroom as she had closed her eyes and let her head fall on Geoffrey's shoulder, her body strangely floating as words drifted to her ears as from some vast distance. "She can't go home tonight… the spare bedroom… she'll be all right, old chap." Lifted lightly, she had been laid down on a large bed, one softer than any she had ever known; had felt it give to Geoffrey's weight, then his body on hers, and she had given herself to him as willingly as on every other occasion when they made love, perhaps more so. Uninhibited by the evening she had spent, the champagne no doubt heightening it, she felt this had to be the best love-making they had ever experienced. In the soft, all-enveloping bed it felt they would never stop.

–

It had been difficult to keep silent about that night, so wonderful if a little hazy. What hurt was to be so devious with William. He didn't deserve to be two-timed, and that was what she was doing, and she hated herself for it.

Being with him was comfortable, unlike with Geoffrey, when she was always on edge, her heart pumping excitedly with the fear that the next time they made love might very well be the last. Common sense told her that they were chalk and cheese, she not of his class, that what they had was tenuous.

How could she reveal to the trusting William what was going on? Sometimes the dilemma solved itself in that, even after that glorious night of Prince Edward's soiree, she still saw her lover so very infrequently that it would be stupid, and unkind, to destroy William's happiness by blabbing all about it. Until Geoffrey finally asked her officially to marry him, she would keep quiet. But would they ever marry?

Ironically, the word never failed to diminish the happiness of being with Geoffrey, and lately it had a bitter ring to it. He had used that word when he had bought her that lovely evening dress in Paris. What was it he had said when she had refused to keep it at home in case her aunt found it and started asking questions?

Geoffrey had laughed. "I'll keep it for you," he had said lightly. "One day I'll give it back to you – when we marry, perhaps."

She had been so excited, but he had never mentioned it again. Said so long ago and just that once, she had come to wonder if she'd imagined the words, never having the courage to raise the issue in case she had. At the back of her mind was the thought that for all their love-making, marriage was the last thing on his mind, that one day he would find a girl of his own class to be his partner in life. He *had* given the dress back to her – that night of the Prince of Wales's soiree. But even as he made love to her, no word of marriage had passed his lips for all she'd given herself totally to him, several times – and at the end of it some strange disembodied instinct told her that she'd conceived. Immediate reaction had been to scoff but two months later instinct proved correct.

Christmas gave her the first indication when her period failed for the second month running. The first week into 1922 brought a more definite sign as one morning, the forerunner of several, she hung over the kitchen sink feeling limp and ill and filled with suppressed terror while her aunt, looking a little mystified, said that she must have eaten something nasty when she'd been celebrating New Year's Eve with that William of hers.

Geoffrey hadn't asked her to the Chelsea Arts Ball, preferring to attend with a crowd of his own sort, and she had felt forgotten. William took her to meet his parents, for the first time ever. It was a quiet do, at midnight a sherry for her and his mother, whisky for the two men. She thought of Geoffrey whooping it up, champagne flowing like water, while in the street outside the Goodridges' small flat, the only celebrations were whistles and cheers welcoming in the New Year.

They were friendly, decent people, William's parents. She had liked them and they had made her welcome, their flat snug and warm against the biting cold outside. There was plenty to eat – leftovers from Christmas – and the conversation was lively, Will's dad churning out a repetoire of jokes, every now and again his wife giving a warning tut should they threaten to get a bit near the knuckle, at which point he would stop, clear his throat, and say, "Sorry – well, 'ave you heard this one? It's clean," as if his guest were a lady of sensitive upbringing. It made Mary smile. It was a cosy evening, yet with her mind running constantly and bitterly towards the one Geoffrey must be having without her, what he would say when she told him her condition and the fear that thought brought, she was glad when the time came to go home.

Out of politeness she hung on until quarter past twelve, then whispered to William, "I ought to be going. My aunt, you know."

"Yes, of course," he said readily, then to his parents, "Mary has to be on her way. She doesn't want to leave her aunt too long."

"Oh, of course." His mother gave her a look of appreciation. "You should 'ave brought 'er along, dear."

"She's been in with our next-door neighbour," Mary said, realising she hadn't referred to her aunt at all, conversation having been quite full.

"That's nice for 'er," said Mrs Goodridge, then her light eyebrows moved up in a query. "You will come again, won't you, dear? We've enjoyed 'aving you. Will tells us so much about you. We look forward ter seeing you again and I expect we will, won't we?"

"Of course you will," put in William. He seemed very certain. "I think you'll be seeing a lot more of her from now on."

It was a form of declaration that couldn't be ignored and, more hastily than she intended, Mary said goodnight to his parents while he went out to the hallway to get their hats and coats. While he was gone Mrs Goodridge came and took her hand, holding it for a few moments longer than appeared necessary, her eyes studying Mary earnestly at the same time, their message unmistakable.

"I'm glad William's picked you, dear. You're a very nice girl. He's a very nice chap, if I do say it myself. You seem so well suited."

Mary smiled wordlessly.

It was Will's father's turn to come forward. He took her lightly by the shoulders and dropped a kiss on her cheek, his bushy moustache pricking her skin. "Look after yourself, Mary. Come to see us soon. Happy New Year, dear."

Again she smiled, wished him one as well.

Will, now in his hat and coat, came back with hers. Putting them on and picking up her handbag, she was asked by his mother if she had everything, and the two of them were seen to the door and out on to the stone landing.

"Take care of her, Will." His mother's voice floated along the landing and down the building's two enclosed flights of stone stairs to the street.

"I certainly will," he called back cheerfully, confidently.

In the street, still full of people continuing to celebrate the new-born 1922, voices above them called down. "Bye-ee! Happy New Year!"

Simultaneously they waved back in reply. "Happy New Year!"

All the way home on the bus William chatted, he doing most of the talking, his arm linked through hers as they sat on a double seat recently vacated by a couple reaching their stop. They, like everyone else getting off at different stops, called out, "Happy New Year!" and received an immediate and hearty response.

William's arm tightened on hers. "Let's hope it brings us a bit of good luck, eh?"

"Yes," she said automatically, her mind elsewhere.

"Did you have a nice time tonight?"

"Yes," she said again.

"They're nice people, don't you think? You did like them?"

"Yes," she said once more.

"I'm glad. I know they liked you. Pity I left it so long before taking you to meet them."

At her door, he kissed her cheek, then tried her lips until she drew away and he stood back, getting the customary message that until a decent girl had a ring on her finger, kisses shouldn't be too passionate in case they led to things for which she might be sorry later.

"Goodnight, Mary. I hope you enjoyed yourself tonght."

"Oh, I did."

"It wouldn't have been much fun for you all on your own with just you and your aunt."

She thought again of Geoffrey and wondered if he might have asked her to go with him to the Arts Ball if Will had not asked her to spend it with him.

But then, he wouldn't have been aware of Will's offer, would he? So she would have been on her own. Again came the bitter knowledge that she was being a fool, kidding herself, jumping at Geoffrey's every request to go to bed with him, knowing it could come to nothing despite all her dreams. And now she was probably pregnant. How could she have let it happen? She dared not think what his reaction would be though she already suspected.

She leaned forward suddenly and kissed William on the lips, taking him by surprise.

"What was that for?"

"For taking me to see your parents," she said. "For making it a lovely evening. And just… for being there for me."

She wanted to say "I love you", but that had the quality of burning her bridges behind her. Besides, in the way she thought of Geoffrey, it wasn't true. She did love Will, could be happy to marry him, might enjoy being made love to by him, but Geoffrey took precedence every time over her feelings for Will.

They stood for a while in a close embrace, she the first to break away as it promised to become more serious. Later she was angry for taking advantage of him in that way; her head had even been playing with the idea of letting him seduce her so he would think himself responsible for this pregnancy.

Her next thought as she lay sleeplessly staring up at the ceiling, across which light from a street lamp cast a thin shaft of washed-out yellow through curtains she had forgotten to draw properly, was that there was no alternative but to seriously consider her condition before it was too late, a thought that brought an instant reaction, a shudder of horror, fear and disbelief. But there was no other way out of what would be seen as disgrace.

Ten

Henry's face was thunderous. He spoke slowly, disparagingly. "You bloody fool, Geoffrey."

"How was I to know it would happen?" His brother's face bore a hangdog expression, one that implored he be let off the leash in any way possible, but Henry had no sympathy for him.

"It usually does when you've not been careful," he said grittily, stubbing out his cigarette in the drawing-room's only ashtray. Mother discouraged smoking in her drawing-room, forbade it altogether in the morning-room where she was wont to sit alone for long hours since the loss of their father. The slightest trace of cigarette – let alone cigar – smoke would have her wrinkling her nose, ordering a maid to push up every one of the tall sash windows that faced east over the extensive grounds, be it August or freezing February as now. But for all her complaining Henry never thought to extinguish a cigarette before entering the room, by now so addicted that most of the time he hardly knew he had one between his fingers.

Geoffrey was pouting. "Perhaps it's not mine. How do I know?"

"Of course it's yours. She's not a girl to sleep with every Tom, Dick and Harry." This he said with conviction, then, in case Geoffrey read more into it than he would have cared to admit, he quickly added, "Anyone looking at her can see that. She's in love with you. She trusted you."

A heaviness had settled in his breast. Why Geoffrey? Why not he? Had Mary Owen cast her lovely hazel eyes at him instead of his brother, he would have taken such care of her that the dilemma that was now occurring would never have been allowed to happen. He would have proposed to her, married her, made her the queen of all he surveyed. They would have had such a life together. But she had looked in Geoffrey's direction, hadn't given himself so much as a glance. And then again, would he, as Geoffrey had so lightly done, have lured her away from that William chap, that waiter who, if he had heard correctly, still took her out occasionally? He didn't think so. He had more scruples than Geoffrey.

Did William know about Geoffrey? Somehow he didn't think so, but rather than see Mary Owen as deceitful – all being fair in love – he saw only Geoffrey as wanting. And now he was fathering the child she was carrying, had been carrying for four months now, leaving very little time left to get rid of it as Geoffrey intimated he would like to have happen.

He took another cigarette from an ornate box, lit it and drew deeply of the smoke, sucking any that escaped back through his nostrils in twin thin streams. His brother, who had been desparately pacing the floor, paused to gaze at him before he too came to help himself to a cigarette.

"What do I do? I can't possibly marry her. I couldn't face Mother with it. God knows what she'll say when she finds out. I don't think I could face anyone right now. What do I say to her... to Mary?"

"When did she tell you?"

"Last night."

"When you were in bed with her, no doubt."

Geoffrey didn't answer. Henry swung away from him in exasperation. What Geoffrey really wanted was his approval of having Mary visit someone who specialised in getting rid of such unwanted problems. The only logical solution, but one Henry couldn't bring himself to endorse, not even with a mere shrug. The idea of her going through that just to appease the finer senses of society, no one even considering her suffering, her loss, was as painful to him as if he were personally involved. He wondered, if Geoffrey asked that of her, would she do it – for him. Obviously she loved him. But so did dozens of young women that he knew of, all clamouring to soothe away that wide-eyed vulnerable look, very much like that of the Prince of Wales who also had women falling at his feet while basking in his charming, lively, self-assured, devil-may-care qualities – all the ones Henry wished he possessed.

People said he was equally as good looking as his brother; they also said he was thoughtful, sober-minded, dependable, but that didn't draw the ladies. He knew he was thought of as one to be trusted. He knew he had a natural aptitude for making people bare their souls before they were even aware of it, he was the ear to many secrets, some quite innocent, some embarrassing, some naughty, some downright evil; the clientele knew nothing would go beyond him. Maybe that was why Geoffrey was telling him all this now in a need to ease his conscience. So would he rather be like Geoffrey? He didn't think so. Compared to some people he'd heard about since taking over Letts, Geoffrey was saintly, but at this moment all Henry saw was an uncaring devil.

"So you don't really love her? She was just a bit of pleasure for the time being, is that it? Now she's in trouble you need to be rid of her, and this child, your child, that she's carrying."

"No, that's not it," Geoffrey countered hotly. "I do love her. That's the problem. But I can't marry her. Mother will have a fit. So will everyone else we know. And think of the publicity when it gets out – bad news always does. 'Letts Owner Has To Marry Pregnant Employee.' What's that going to do to our reputation?"

"Hell to our reputation!" Henry exploded – but he knew it mattered. With something like this, royals would withdraw their patronage. The rest, taking their cue from them, would stay away, go elsewhere. There were any number of high-class restaurants in London, just around the comer in fact: Wiltons and the Ritz were both within spitting distance. Just when they were lifting off the ground, after their father's death had almost destroyed the place, Geoffrey with his selfishness threatened to bring it crashing down. Strange how one small indiscretion could generate such repercussions.

Such fine people we all are, Henry found himself sneering, *such small gods when it comes to considering others.* He found himself jolted back to the fact that he too had been guilty, had been thinking of himself and what this would do to his livelihood. What about Mary? He knew he ought to say to Geoffrey, "You'll have to give her the money for an abortion", yet what about her?

"It's your problem," he blurted. "You sort it out." And, stubbing out his cigarette in the ashtray, he strode from the room, wishing he could stride as easily from the sickness that had risen up inside him when he thought of Mary.

–

The glow of the previous street lamp receding, the next one some way off as yet, William took advantage of the gloom to put an arm around Mary's waist.

Tonight he was feeling particularly certain of himself. The show with Harry Lauder had been good. Mary had laughed at Lauder's comical songs, although lately she'd become rather solemn and distant. He thought it might be the drawing out of this association of theirs with still no ring to show for it, so he decided to propose to her this evening as they said goodnight, and tell her they would look for a ring next Saturday. It was bound to cheer her.

All this saving up; it couldn't go on forever. But he knew what she'd say: she would purse her lips, all concerned, and remind him of the million men on the dole queue. He could hear her saying it: "What if you lost your job, Will? It's happening to so many." But he could laugh away her fears. Mr Eustace, the head waiter, had lately been praising his work. And a man whose work is praised would hardly be out on his ear the very next week. Indeed, the word had got to Mr Henry's ear who had stopped one day on his way through the restaurant to tell him personally that he was glad to see him doing well. So now, a sight more certain of the future than before, he felt confident enough to tell Mary they would buy the long-awaited engagement ring next Saturday. She would be so relieved.

"Enjoyed yourself tonight?" he asked.

"It was really nice," she replied, watching their feet as they walked slowly, their shadows moving ahead of them but already fading. Soon they would reappear behind them as they got nearer to the next street lamp. He wanted to stop and kiss her before then.

"And that was a lovely box of chocolates," she sighed. "Bit lavish though, don't you think?"

"Ah," he said contentedly. "Well, it is rather a special evening." It was now or never. "Mary," he began, but she interrupted him.

"I've got a bit of news for you," she said, and racing on, added, "I'm not sure if you'll be pleased for me or not."

"Whatever it is," he said, putting aside talk of the ring, "I'm sure it'll be all right with me."

"I don't know," she said, doubt creeping into her tone. "You see, you know about all this foot-and-mouth epidemic that's sweeping through the country? Well, it's upsetting the meat trade and there's a big meeting in Birmingham of everyone concerned with the catering trade. Mr Geoffrey is having to go. Mr Henry needs to stay here to look after things. Well, Mr Geoffrey will need someone to take notes for him at this meeting and he's asked me if I'd go with him. It wouldn't be for long."

The information came out in a gabble so that Mr Geoffrey's name was almost submerged within it, but William was aware of an uncomfortable sensation. Something the head chef had said to him, so long ago that he'd long since shrugged it off, almost managed to forget it with he and Mary still going steady together, now came flooding back.

"Is anyone else going?" he asked, his voice brittle, the kiss he was going to give her abandoned.

"There'll be lots of people there."

"I mean, from Letts."

"I think they've asked the other girl who works in the office, but I'm not sure if her parents will let her go. If not, one of the lads will."

"What about your aunt? What happens to her if you leave her?"

"Oh, our neighbour will look after her. They're quite thick, you know."

It seemed Mary had got this all sorted out, all without telling him. "When were you asked?" he taxed.

"A couple of days ago." she said quickly. "But I haven't had a chance to see you until now."

"You could have told me earlier this evening."

"And spoil it all?"

It was spoiled now. He should be telling her that he wasn't keen to have her go – that he would rather she told Geoffrey Lett to find someone else. But would that jeopardise her job?

Then, should it matter if it did? After all, when they married she'd be giving up her job anyway. Married women didn't work, not in offices, and if he couldn't look after her on his salary, he'd be a poor husband. On the other hand, they couldn't be married for at least six months – the cost of the engagement ring would take a large chunk out of his post office book – and her earnings until then would go some way towards the wedding and a good start in some nice little rented accommodation.

He walked in silence for a while, his arm around her waist. Finally he came to a conclusion.

"How long will you be away?" he asked.

She thought for a moment. "I don't really know. A week." She seemed genuinely upset, her voice trembling, and his arm tightened around her.

A week wasn't all that long. Often they weren't able to meet for a whole week ordinarily, his shifts long, his break times erratic now that there was late-night dancing and even a cabaret in the restaurant with lots of wealthy and well-known people jazzing around on the small dance floor. Thirsty, they demanded a continuous supply of drinks and tipped well. His share of the pooled gratuities, small as it was, helped swell his savings. He couldn't afford not to do overtime.

"Very well, darling," he said at last. "I can put up with not seeing you for a week."

He would put off telling her about the engagement ring until next time, but he kissed her instead, delighted that she returned his kiss whole-heartedly – desperately, he would have said if he hadn't known better.

–

The place looked very expensive. In fact she had guessed it would be. Geoffrey would not have stinted on this, the most important thing ever to happen to her. He would want every care lavished on her, no slip-ups. Yet she shivered with apprehension and clung to his hand even more tightly as they sat on a sofa in the tasteful reception area.

"It's so quiet," she whispered, the silence compelling her to lower her voice.

She felt the pressure of his hand around hers, comforting, reassuring. "Don't let it worry you. I'm assured they're very kind, very understanding. You'll be all right, darling. These private clinics are wonderfully good."

He spoke as though this was a jaunt and she would have such fun.

"You'll be fine, darling," he said again. Yet still she shivered. All the way to this Middlesex clinic she had felt abnormally cold, and it hadn't all to do with bitter February weather. Geoffrey had tucked a car rug tenderly about her knees, for all the car windows stayed closed except for when he had put out an arm to signal his intentions to other drivers before manoevring. Then a blast of snow-laden air would smite her so that she would pull the car rug closer around her. The cold seemed to have eaten into her very bones, but she knew it was not so much from the weather as from fear.

It felt as if they had been sitting here in this reception for hours, though of course that wasn't true.

Someone had come out and taken her particulars, and she had seen the doctor in charge so that he could explain to her what would be done. She had come back more terrified than she'd already been. Finally the time came for Geoffrey to leave, saying that he would come back later to visit her – she was staying in for five days.

It was for the best, Geoffrey had told her. He had explained in gentle words how impossible it would be to keep the baby. She was over four months gone already; it would soon be noted that he was marrying her while she was pregnant. She hadn't taken heart this time from the word "marriage". Then he'd explained that should she get pregnant again, he'd see to it their child would not be labelled illegitimate and from this she did take heart, and, lighter with the knowledge that they would be married before there was any likelihood of another child, she had consented for this pregnancy to be terminated. But now, sitting here, waiting all this time, she was becoming terribly afraid.

"Don't be," Geoffrey told her, his hand tightening over hers. "There's no better clinic in the country. No expense has been spared, darling." His voice was a little shaky – she knew he cared for her.

"I wish you didn't have to leave me, Geoffrey."

"I'll visit you tomorrow. By then it will all be over and you'll be as right as rain."

Without this inside me, she reflected as she watched him roar away in his car. Being without this inside her brought a small pang to her heart, even though she'd never felt a real bond as any expectant mother would – only heartache. Instinct had told her that what had happened to her could have driven Geoffrey away from her. It was that which prompted her to do as he bade, get back to normal, and – she knew this last from the way he kissed her so tenderly, concernedly, as he said goodbye to her – they continue as before, but this time with marriage in mind.

"We're ready for you, my dear."

The nurse was standing over her, the high fee for this particular patient making her voice soft and polite. The patient would not be referred to as "Miss", merely "my dear"; must not be made to feel herself under pressure or stigmatised in any way; must not be given any cause to complain to the man who had brought her in, who had handed the large cheque to the clinic and who expected value for his money.

"If you would like to come this way, my dear?"

Mary got up and, feeling unexpectedly meek, followed the nurse who smiled in a friendly way and cooed encouragement.

"I am sure you will be quite comfortable. You have a private room. No one will bother you."

Leading the way, she opened a door to a bright and cheerful little room containing a narrow bed with pink sheets, a dressing-table, a wardrobe, a sink in the comer with a mirror above it and a cupboard under it, a small chair and table with reading matter and a small bowl of fruit on it, and pink curtains at the window. Across the bed lay a white silk dressing-gown and a cotton nightie – a gift, Mary realised with a surge of love, from Geoffrey.

"If you would like to unpack your things," the nurse was saying, pulling back the cover of the bed so that Mary could slip into it when she had finished, "just ring the bell there. Someone will come in to see if you have all you need, though I'm afraid we cannot give you any tea or anything to eat until after your operation. Now don't worry about a thing. I promise, you will know nothing about it at all. When you wake up you will feel fine, and then we will give you a cup of tea and a little round of toast. Later you will have a small meal. In a moment someone will give you a tablet to make you drowsy, and you will know nothing more."

I won't even know if I died, came the thought, almost muffled panic. She had never had an operation in her life, nor even been in hospital, except when she had been a baby, she'd been told, with scarlet fever; but she could remember nothing of that, only that she had survived the disease completely unscathed. If she died during this operation, she would never know.

Mary bit her lip, having smiled bravely at the nurse and the woman having closed the door softly behind her. Automatically she began to unpack the nightie she had brought, her make-up, comb and brush and a change of clothing. Carefully she put the things where they had to go, then sat on the bed, her knees drawn up to her chin.

Between her legs she was aware of her private parts. Soon someone would be probing there, inserting something… doing something to her… She felt her insides begin to creep. *Oh, Geoffrey, come back for me – I can't face this alone. I can't go through with this.*

She became aware of a smell above the freshness of the room, at first a hardly detectable smell of anti-septic… no, anaesthetic, strong now, the sort of smell that floods dentists' rooms. It was the smell of fear, the smell of terror. Panic began to mount. Unreasonable panic, she knew, for they had told her she would know nothing.

Knowing nothing or not, Mary suddenly knew she couldn't go through with this. Couldn't. Her breath was becoming harsh and laboured, cramping her heart, strangling in her throat, her throat tight-ening, hysteria taking hold.

Madly, she pressed the bell the nurse had indicated. Somewhere came a faint buzz. No one came. She pressed again. Still no one. They had left her to die of this terrible fear that was consuming her. Mary heard her voice crying out, begging someone to come. Frantically she pressed the bell again and again. The door opened.

"My dear, what is the matter?" She couldn't recognise the woman; it could have been the nurse who had so politely, kindly, shown her to the room, but her terror-filled eyes saw only a woman looking at her. There was a buzzing, whining sound that seemed to be inside her head, and the sound of her own voice crying, "Get me out of here! I want to leave!"

"You can't at the moment, dear."

"I don't want to stay here. I want to see Geoffrey."

Hands were holding her, pushing her on to her back on the bed. "You're just a little frightened. Everything will be all right, my dear. You must try to relax…"

"No!" With unexpected strength, Mary pushed the arms off her, flung herself from the bed. "I mean it – I want to leave here. I'm not going through with it."

The woman had relaxed, stood back. Now Mary saw it was the same nurse who had shown her to her room. The pale features had taken on a placid, appeasing expression. "We will not make you do what you don't want to do, Mary." The hands moved towards her, freshly scrubbed palms with the look of two soft cushions facing towards her in a small appeal. One hand dropped to indicate the chair and table. "If you would sit down, Mary, and calm yourself." It was as though she were addressing the insane. "I'm sure in a little while you will feel better."

Mary did as she was told. She did feel calmer but no less determined. There was no way she would let herself be mauled by some unseen doctor. She wanted Geoffrey. She had made up her mind: she would go away, find lodgings somewhere and have the baby. Oddly, it seemed infinitely more acceptable than allowing this clinical intrusion into her insides.

"I want to see Mr Lett," she said stubbornly, in charge of herself once more. The nurse nodded, her face cold, no longer friendly.

"Very well, Miss Owen. We will see if we can contact him for you."

Leaving Mary sitting on the chair, she went swiftly out, closing the door not quite so softly behind her. Money would have to be handed back should the client leave, but there was little they could do about that.

–

In the small hotel room, the curtains closed to ease Mary's reddened eyes, Geoffrey held her to him.

He had never seen anyone in such a state as she had been in when he came to the clinic. She had thrown herself into his arms in tears. He had reasoned with her, tried to make her see sense, all to no avail. There was no moving her – she would not go through with it, and between gulping tears had said she would pay him back the money he had spent on her.

He had smiled at that, despite his frustration. Where would she find five hundred pounds? The offer had wrung his heart, something it wasn't used to. Then it had done something totally unexpected

– seemed to swell as all the love he had ever known was poured into it in one stream. Quite suddenly he knew he could never let Mary go, that no other girl would ever fill his heart as she was doing.

Making his excuses to the clinic, he'd waved away the reluctant offer to return his money and had taken Mary, huddled in the coat he had collected with the rest of her belongings, out into the biting February wind and into his car. From there he'd driven to this little hotel in which he now held her close.

"Mary," he whispered against her ear. "I am going to marry you. We'll stay here the night, and tomorrow we'll go back to London, get you some decent accommodation. I'll get a special licence and we'll get married."

Impulsive, yes, but the way he felt at this moment, who cared? His whole being was warmed by the love mounting inside him for this girl as she flung herself into his arms. If he were to put her aside now, his whole life would be as nothing. He wanted Mary, at this moment wanted her for the rest of his life. Only by making her his wife could he have that.

The following morning, after they had slept, he with an arm around her all night, her head cradled against his shoulder, the loss of feeling in that arm nothing to the way he still felt for the vulnerable sleeping girl, he kissed her lightly on the forehead. She opened her eyes, blinked and smiled at him.

Three days later they married.

Geoffrey sent Henry a telegram, telling him of the fact and informing him that he and his new wife would be having a short honeymoon and that he would see Henry on his return. Meantime, would Henry break the news to Mother, gently?

The next thing would be to find a nice flat for Mary, away from anyone who knew him. No one must know of the baby. Tongues mustn't be allowed to wag. When it was bom, he'd find a nurse for it, and when Mary was strong enough he would take her out and about. They'd have a wonderful time socialising, she in the finest and most fashionable clothes, and no one need know about the baby until the shock of his sudden marriage was long forgotten. It was a fine plan. Mary would go along with it, he knew. What girl wouldn't?

Eleven

"What are you doing, darling?"

Geoffrey looked up from the dressing-table. "Writing to Henry," he said, "at greater length than my telegram telling him of our marriage."

It felt strange thinking of her old employer in terms of "Henry" rather than "Mr Henry" – now her brother-in-law, and that felt even stranger.

Lying in bed in the hotel he had chosen for the time being, Mary gave a small shiver of delight. "I hope he'll be pleased," she murmered lazily. "I hope your mother will too."

"Don't lay bets on it," he said, his voice muffled as he bent his head again to his letter so that she hardly caught what he said.

But it didn't matter. She stretched slowly and luxuriously to her full length beneath the soft covers, slim arms raised above her head to curl around the top edge of the lacy pillow.

Mrs Geoffrey Lett. A few months ago, who'd have believed it? She'd have liked the whole world to know, but there was no one to tell. Married by special licence in a little registry office, her aunt informed of her condition, having been required to give her consent, her niece being still only twenty. Odd that Aunt Maud, whose faculties were somewhat tenuous, was required to give consent, but there was no other relative.

She thought of her aunt and hoped she was all right. Worried about her at the time of her reluctant trip to that awful house, she'd asked Mrs Trench to keep an eye on her.

Mrs Trench had instantly suggested Mary's aunt stay with her while Mary was away. "For as long as you like, lovey," she'd said, her trained nurse's eye having already noted the condition which so far had escaped the notice of others.

Looking after Aunt Maud was right up Mrs Trench's street. A lonely though robust sixty-something, she had retired from nursing these last few years. Mrs Trench might have been pretty in her youth but a dry skin that wrinkled quickly and the way in which she scragged back her grey hair in a tight old-fashioned bun made her look more in her seventies even though she had the energy of a woman fifteen years younger. Her husband having died of tuberculosis ten years into their marriage, she had taken an interest in midwifery becoming quite skilled and training at the Nightingale School for Nurses. When the Great War came she'd cared for wounded soldiers but had been retired when the war finished, by then too old for civilian hospitals. "They put you out to grass once they've got all they can get out of you," she took pleasure in lamenting, more than happy to take on her neighbour for as long as Mary wanted.

Geoffrey had paid her generously for her pains, four shillings a day - almost a man's wages — which had made her eyes gleam while she protested that she would have done it out of pure neighbourliness.

With nothing to worry her, Mary sighed contentedly. It might not have been the wedding she'd have wanted – a simple registry office, she in a cream outfit with a tiny posy of pink flowers, he in just an ordinary suit, the two witnesses they would probably never see again, wishing them well – but at least Geoffrey had made an honest woman of her, as the saying went. Her husband was a man of means and of high social standing, he and his brother owners of a well-known and thriving restaurant business: why quibble about a mere registry office wedding? She was content.

Last night in this little hotel, she and Geoffrey had consummated their marriage, tenderly, he careful of the child inside her, his cautious love-making filling her with far greater desire than at any of their wilder moments. She knew she had done the right thing. Something told her that had she gone through with the horrible business in the clinic, she and Geoffrey would have parted company, he being relieved of that burden. Oddly, though, she felt no sense of recrimination, only joy and amazement that, the baby saved, Geoffrey's love for her had grown even stronger.

"What have you said in the letter?" she asked.

For an answer he picked it up and read: "Dear Mother, I am sending this letter to you through Henry to whom I sent my telegram as I feel he may be able to soften the blow I expect my news must have dealt you. Her name is Mary and she is the most wonderful person in the whole world…"

He looked up to smile across at her, then went on, "It all happened so quickly. I've discovered that there is no one else in the world I would rather be with, so I went ahead and married her. I expect you'll be disappointed that I didn't introduce her to you beforehand, but I'll tell you more about it when I return home. We're off on a short honeymoon and I am sure Henry will be able to carry on without me for that while. The business doesn't need the two of us.

"Mother will be furious, of course," he said as he signed the letter with a flourish. "But I don't think I would have wanted an official church wedding and a huge reception full of people I don't know and care even less about."

Mary wasn't listening. She sat up straight in bed. "Honeymoon?"

"Of course," he said smoothly. "What about an Atlantic cruise?"

She was aware of her mouth having fallen open. "A… a…You mean on a ship?"

She suddenly felt the weight of her own ignorance as he chuckled, the laugh casual and mature as though cruising the Atlantic was nothing to him. But an eager gleam in his eyes betrayed him. Underneath he was as excited by the idea as she was. Still an immature boy – twenty-one two months ago, a grand coming-of-age party having been thrown in his honour, he'd told her – this would be a great adventure for him as much as for her. It made her feel much better that he didn't see her as ignorant after all.

Dropping his letter on the dressing-table, he came and sat beside her on the bed with such force that the springs bounced.

"I can book tickets on the *Mauretania*," he said. "Fastest thing afloat – crosses the Atlantic in something like six days. We'll go first class." *Savoir-faire* melting completely, he had become like an excited little boy on his first outing. "What d'you say, Mrs Lett, to a cruise to New York and back?"

Mary drew in a gasp that was a mixture of delight at the sheer sound of her new name, disbelief at the honeymoon he was suggesting, and joy that he could love her so much that money was no object.

"Oh… oh, Geoffrey… oh, y-yes," she stammered, anything else she might have said smothered by his lips, his kiss far from immature.

–

Henry hadn't shown the telegram to his mother. Head of the household now, it was he to whom Atkinson brought the message. Henry thanked providence that his mother hadn't seen it first as he'd opened it casually only to stand transfixed by what it contained.

Ripping the thing up after reading it, he'd dropped it into the wicker waste-paper basket beside the writing desk that his father had once sat at, already wondering how the hell he was going to break Geoffrey's news to Mother. So abrupt, so thoughtless. Geoffrey cared only for himself. All right, so the girl was pregnant and Geoffrey was doing the right thing by her, but it should never have been allowed to happen in the first place. This would kill their mother.

But that was being a little over the top. Mother was made of sterner stuff. Even so, how did one break that sort of news to a woman of such high standards?

Henry had spent the rest of the day in turmoil. Perhaps Geoffrey would write at length once he was settled. Perhaps that might soften the blow a little. Henry held fire for another twenty-four hours, and sure enough a letter arrived the following day. Intercepting Atkinson in the hall before Mother could realise the afternoon post had arrived, he agitatedly sifted through the few letters on the salver, plucking up the one he recognised with Geoffrey's handwriting.

"Is that the post, dear?" His mother came into the hall dressed in an old-fashioned afternoon gown reaching to her ankles. Her face was tired, her movements listless. Even her voice sounded disinterested.

She was smoking a cigarette in a long ivory holder. Since the death of her husband she had taken up the habit. Henry was glad. It calmed her.

Now he stuffed Geoffrey's letter into his smoking-jacket pocket. "Do you want to look through them, Mother?"

"Not at the moment, dear." There was still that air of detachment from things real about her. "You can give me those that are for me later on."

With that she went back towards the morning-room, her favourite room. The door closed gently and moments later Henry heard her putting on the gramophone and recognised the plaintive strains of his father's favourite record, the last one he had ever bought. "I found my love in Avalon, beside the bay... I left my love in Avalon... and sailed away... I dream of her and Avalon..."

It had been nearly a year since his father's death. Anniversaries. This one would be coming round soon to renew his mother's pain, if indeed it had ever ceased. Henry turned back to the salver Atkinson held before him in white gloved hands, nodding to him to take it into the study. Following at a leisurely pace, for not even Atkinson must realise how agitated he felt, he waited until the butler had gone before taking the envelope from his pocket and opening it.

It was as he had suspected: full of apologies, explanations, entreaties to be understood. Geoffrey was all for himself, never once paused to find out how others felt. Geoffrey would always fall on his feet. And now Geoffrey had Mary and would have her for himself for the rest of his life. She would want for nothing, he knew that. Geoffrey knew how to treat a woman. And the baby? Geoffrey would be a good father, of that he was sure, for all his other shortcomings. Mary was a lucky girl. If only she had been his…

He turned his mind to his mother. He must go and break the news of Geoffrey's marriage. She'd be hurt, confused, maybe in that order, lastly furious at his running roughshod over protocol and family values. She would put her hands to her lips in shame and misery at his conduct. Henry could almost hear her saying, "How could he? Your poor dear father dead hardly these twelve months, and this is how he treats his memory, treats us who are still grieving. No word, just… married! Your brother has no concern for any but himself. I can never forgive him."

But she would forgive him, for he was her flesh and blood and she his mother. Mothers forgive most things. Whether she would accept his wife was another matter. Mary coming from a lower class; it would take time – years – before she'd be accepted, if at all. And Mother would be within her rights; all the love in the world that Geoffrey had for Mary could not make his mother like her. Henry's heart ached for Mary's pain when she finally realised her position in this family.

"Avalon" ceased then began again as Henry went out into the hall.

-

The honeymoon was nearly over. It had gone by so quickly, like a dream. The start of it seemed so far away now, that in itself no more than a dream now.

At Southampton, blindly following Geoffrey at an urgent pace, their porter trundling their baggage on a small hand truck, she had been surrounded by bustle and noise. As they emerged on to the quayside, her breath had been taken away by the great hull of the *Mauretania* rearing over her, above that the glaring white superstructure and four red and black funnels. Dwarfed by it, she'd followed behind Geoffrey and their porter up the first-class gangway to be swallowed by the liner like a morsel in the mouth of a great whale.

She couldn't remember being shown to their cabin, she had been in such a daze. She had imagined some poky little place, maybe slung with two hammocks. But the sight that greeted her she would never forget. A large room, all bright and cheerful, with a bathroom going off it; a double bed with frilled peach floral covers; matching curtains at the portholes; a dressing-table with a long mirror; wardrobes, a fluffy peach carpet, a small round table and two chairs; on the table a vase of flowers, and on a bedside cabinet an ice bucket with a bottle of champagne and a note that said in large letters: "Congratulations and welcome to your Honeymoon Suite".

"Oh, Geoffrey," Mary recalled herself gasping. "Oh, it's lovely!"

They'd gone on deck as the *Mauretania* glided away from the quayside after what had seemed like hours of waiting before finally moving off. Far below, the oval blobs of faces looking up had called farewell to those they knew. No one was there to see her and Geoffrey off but it hadn't mattered. Leaning over the rail, she had waved back as frantically as any down there on the quay, joining in the excitement, all the time her bemused mind saying over and over again, *This is me – me!*, still unable to grasp that it could actually be *her* on that huge liner.

Soon due to return to the ship, small things were coming back to her: the warm oily smell of the docks mixed with a variety of other smells: stale produce, squashed fruit and rotting vegetables. She remembered the first rumble of the ship's engines starting up, vibrating through her feet and up to her head, threatening to shake the vessel and her to pieces. She wondered with dismay whether this was to be with her across the whole Atlantic? But of course it had eventually given way to a low throbbing which she had soon got so used to that she forgot it was going on at all.

There had been clanging bells, rattling of huge chains, thick hawsers thrown off to splash in the flat water, the great leviathan turning slowly and majestically with foam boiling, all finally settling down as the docks moved further away, then the land going by, the hills of Dorset and Devon moving steadily away, getting smaller and smaller, then England at last sinking into the sea, excitement diminished. The passengers going about their own pursuits, she and Geoffrey had made the most of their honeymoon by drinking up the complimentary champagne and, a little tipsy, recementing their marriage. She remembered the fresh tang of the ocean afterwards, the air like nothing she had ever smelled before. There were snatches of other memories: a soft sough of the ship's bows cutting through the smooth water – they'd had fine weather all the way, not sunny but calm, the water like oil. The swell had initially made her feel just a little queasy though that went after a while, proving her a good sailor. She remembered the babble of people's voices, the piano music coming from the restaurant and the lounge, and in the ballroom an orchestra playing, and the smell wafting in now and again of beautifully cooked food mixed with the ever-present sooty odour that sank down from the funnels. She recalled the wind in her face reminding her that they were romping along as fast as a moderate car's pace, and the wake they left behind them stringing itself out to the empty horizon like a long cloud on the sea. So much of it remembered, but so much of it feeling now as in a dream.

She hoped that she would be able to savour the journey home with more awareness. Her only regret about the outward passage was that the entire journey had been spent in the daze of an ordinary girl who'd not so much as had a seaside holiday before, but for a day trip to Southend. She'd had to pinch herself time and time again to make sure it was all real. That, and the lingering feeling that she still didn't quite belong, was still not quite accepted as Geoffrey's wife.

She was still uneasy mingling with people who only a month ago she would have considered to be above her. Overawed by the impressive passenger list, she'd discovered that travelling on that great ship with her had been several titled people as well as two well-known film stars and a celebrated Broadway singer returning home. It all but stifled her seeing such people at tables hardly a stone's throw from hers and Geoffrey's in the huge, ornate first-class dining-room so that she could hardly draw breath, much less eat the wonderful food put before her. Geoffrey, however, being well versed in the catering profession, took it all in his stride, as if he were thirty-one and not twenty-one. She'd watched with pride and awe as he surveyed the dishes, inclined his head knowledge-ably and reflectively sipped the wine offered for his opinion before gracefully accepting.

By the time they had docked in New York they had made friends with two other couples – not the most celebrated ones, but young like themselves and wealthy enough. Mary had slowly learned to be more at ease, finding herself accepted. One couple came from Devon and, like she and Geoffrey, were newly weds and a little shy about it which in a way helped Mary feel a little more certain of herself. The other couple, married these two years they said, came from Surrey and were more sure of themselves. Mary leaned towards the more rustic Louise and Bertie, but even Lyndon and Barbara did not sport too much affectation apart from being utterly modem and were fun to be with.

Time here in New York had simply flown. So much to do: theatres, mostly going in a group, in a strange land needing to stick together like castaways on some uncharted island; likewise safe hotel night-clubs – the Plaza's Persian Room, the Empire Room at the Waldorf. During the day they'd discovered Central Park and all it had to offer despite it being winter – children snowballing, sledding on its snowy slopes, skidding along home-made slides. At Wollman Memorial Rink, Geoffrey had helped her learn to skate with many a shriek from her and laughter from the others. They'd done some sightseeing, this time on their own, each couple with their own idea of what they wanted to see in this vast city of monuments and museums. Such a lot to see, hardly time to see it all, so much left out, but there had been shopping.

She and Geoffrey on their own, going into wonderful shops, she still hardly able to believe it wasn't all a dream as they went up in elevators and stepped out on to the various floors for her to buy hats, shoes, lingerie; dresses that caused her too to automatically glide as fashionable women did when they moved – as though she had been used to it all her life.

She found out how to pour herself into a *diamante-decorated* crepe de Chine evening dress by Worth, her still slim figure and small bust just made for today's fashion, and wore it to her first hotel night-club, glorying in having heads turn and knowing that she was beautiful. Her stomach revealing only the slightest bulge, a flowing gauze scarf hiding that, her condition was such that, as with all expectant women, there was a special glow about her. In her case it was added to by the opulence of her new life, an expensive hair-do, good make-up, and her overwhelming gratitude towards and love for Geoffrey.

It being late February, and the weather far colder than in England, he had bought her a Persian lamb coat into which she sank cosily. Geoffrey thought of everything, even the pair of "Ritz Imperials", up-to-the-minute rubber gaiters that fitted over evening shoes to protect them from the wet pavements where the snow had melted underfoot. For five days out of seven it had snowed, the remaining two being dull and overcast. But it didn't matter. She was with Geoffrey – an arctic blizzard, a full hurricane, the world coming to an end could not have spoiled it for her.

Bad weather or not, New York was a breathtaking place, at times a little alarming. It was hard for eyes and senses to adjust to towering buildings; brash, noisy, crowded streets; everyone seeming to be in a perpetual hurry to be somewhere else, ignoring the newly arrived passengers from the great *Mauretania*. But, Geoffrey told her, New York had taken in arrivals from every corner of the earth all its life, so why should it stop for them?

By the end of their stay she'd become a tiny bit disenchanted by it all. True, everything glittered and sparkled; Times Square and Broadway were lit by a confusion of animated electric signs that reflected off the wet pavements in a glorious shimmer, a million jewels at her feet. Yet people hurrying by with heads down saw nothing, distracted by their own need of privacy as they leapt on and off single-decker buses or into the rattling, blaring taxis. Outside the Plaza horse-drawn hansom cabs clattered; everywhere music boomed; no one dreamed of speaking quietly, instead shrieking as if the listener were fifty yards away. Caught up in the bustle, Mary had learned to be private, her eyes only for Geoffrey. She too took little note of those around her, bent on their own pursuits, or of the occasional shadowy bundle huddled in a doorway, or an alley close to the warmth of a street grill that issued steam into the chill air. She learned to ignore the passing figure that dragged its feet, bent into a threadbare coat against the cold

– she, who had herself felt the ache of poverty and unemployment only a few years back, forgot, as often with those newly risen in the world, to think of the joylessness so recently left behind, saw only her own glittering future, perhaps fearing some sense of guilt should she pause to reflect on the less fortunate. Like the New Yorkers it was easier to avert her eyes, even if conscious of doing so, for life was so rushed, too rushed to stop and think. And the crowds helped take her mind off it.

Private parties were a wow! It appeared that Lyndon and Barbara had friends in Manhattan, and they had invited Mary, Geoffrey and the other couple to two on Park Avenue which turned out to be quite large. Prohibition being of little concern as long as no one tried to buy drink outside, they got "kinda wild", as one New Yorker remarked. Jazz was far more the rage than at home, and Mary, leaping and gyrating at the Cotton Club in Harlem, had found a talent she hadn't known she possessed. Geoffrey had been hard put to keep up with her or keep her to himself.

"I don't like you making free and easy on the dance floor with every man you see," he'd told her several times, and she had prinked herself all the more, happily enjoying his jealousy, it proving his love for her, her prior and brief disillusion with New York diminishing.

Now it was all over. They were heading home. But there was no need to think drearily of that awhile, with life on board resuming its endless round of fun – as good as, if not better than on the way out for she was now at ease.

Now able to vie confidently with the next woman – in this, at least, New York having taught her a thing or two – Mary Lett now knew herself the wife of a prominent and successful London restaurant owner, every bit as good as any one of them.

There was much to keep passengers happy on the homeward voyage, especially the few shops that, small though they were, stocked high-priced, up-to-the-minute fashions for wealthy first-class passengers who would not dream of buying anything less. As if Mary hadn't enough clothes, she fell in love with an exquisite evening dress in shot green brocade and silver lame with dramatic slashed sleeves that she could see would fan out as she walked or danced, complete with one of the new bandeaux in matching green and *diamante* that so suited her new short hairstyle.

Catching sight of it as she and Geoffrey strolled arm in arm through the shopping area prior to the Captain's Dinner the second night out, she pulled back abruptly as the dress caught her eye, and clutched Geoffrey's arm excitedly.

"Oh, darling, isn't that exquisite? Can't you just see me in that?"

Geoffrey smiled indulgently. "Don't you think you've enough clothes?"

"Nothing that everyone hasn't already seen. I simply can't wear the same thing I wore to the Captain's Dinner on the way out. People would notice."

On the way out, her dresses had been conservative, her tastes still modest. She now felt ashamed of them, New York having done something to her that was now beyond repair. "Oh, darling, it's a dream," she pleaded. "Oh please, Geoffrey, can't I have it?"

He bit his lip over a hasty reckoning of resources which were getting alarmingly slim, he having somewhat underestimated the cost of this honeymoon. But his restaurant was booming. He'd recuperate his expenses in no time. He relented, and seconds later Mary was trying the dress on without one glance at the price tag as the glorious garment slipped over her figure as though made for it.

In a week her tiny bulge had grown quite pronounced, she noticed. Staring at it with dismay that morning as she stood naked before the mirror of the dressing-table in her cabin, Geoffrey had come to stand behind her to see her body from her viewpoint and had put his hands over the tiny swelling.

"It suits you," he said. "Makes you look quite seductive."

She hadn't prinked and blushed, hadn't replied. What would he say when she was seven months, all bloated and distended and half the size of a house?

But the Molyneux dress, cut to drape, did a marvellous job of hiding what showed at the moment.

On that point alone it vindicated the extravagance and Mary closed her eyes to the cheque Geoffrey passed to the woman who had attended them.

She wore it at the Captain's Dinner, the resultant turning of heads proof enough that once she'd had this baby, she, on Geoffrey's arm, would virtually take London by storm. She would be the talk of the town and he would gain even more patronage because of it. She intended to see Geoffrey the most talked about, the most seen, the most sought-after man in London.

Thus she dreamed as she attended on-board parties, moved sylph-like through the ornate first-class dining-room to their table, enthusiastically participated in endless deck games or lounged in comfortable chairs on the upper deck. Out of the cold wind, she lay snuggled in her Persian lamb coat, a deep-crowned hat pulled down over her ears and a cosy plaid wool rug pulled up to them for all that the sun shone quite warmly approaching England. Later, and in the huge, domed first-class ballroom in one of her beautiful ankle-length evening dresses, she was aware of eyes turned again and again in her direction. She was learning her part well.

It was good to see Geoffrey looking on with pride and in their honeymoon suite they made love every night of the five-and-a-half-day crossing, he less intimidated by the baby she carried as it began to appear that love-making wouldn't harm her.

In all this time they hadn't once discussed the future, too full of each other. Now, during the last night before docking at Southampton, Geoffrey spoke of it as she lay in his arms.

"When we get back," he said, "I'll have to find a flat for us."

That was fine; she was happy with that. But he went on, "The only thing that worries me is that I might not be able to be with you every single day for a while."

A small void immediately made itself known somewhere inside her as she worried that, having married her, having had the most fantastic honeymoon with her, Geoffrey was now content to leave her to herself, his duty done. That couldn't be.

"You don't mean to leave me in a flat all on my own?" she protested.

Geoffrey smiled. "Well, I shall get you a maid and a cook." But when she looked at him, glum and scared, his face broke into a grin and he added quickly, "And when the baby is bom we'll have a nurse to look after it while you and I go out and about and enjoy ourselves. You'll meet all sorts of people, Mary, I promise."

The relief that washed over her as he kissed her, gently, tenderly, with all the love that she realised afresh he possessed for her, was itself almost as excruciating as the dismay a moment before.

"I do love you, Geoffrey," she whispered. "I love you so very much."

"And I love you," he said, lightly, and kissed her again.

Twelve

Henry glared at his brother from across the library. "So you've hidden her away."

"I haven't hidden her away," came the affronted reply, prompting Henry to make a great play of staring around the library, gazing past his brother to the wall beyond and saying with flippant sarcasm, "Well, I can't see her."

The remark was childish and not what he had intended to say, but Henry was angry. His brother had floated in minutes ago, brightly asking where Mother was as though he hadn't a care in the world. No thought to how she would receive him. As a matter of fact she had already seen him driving up in a smart new Calcott – Geoffrey always had over-expensive tastes – and had withdrawn to the morning-room, her face stiff, saying that she would consider whether or not to greet him when he felt inclined to come and see her. Henry knew what that meant. Geoffrey would have to tread carefully in regard to the marriage alone. In what way would he approach the even more important matter of Mary's pregnancy, if he dared to do so at all? Henry could see his present bravado letting him down.

"I've got us got a flat," Geoffrey was saying doggedly.

"You mean you've got *her* a flat. Bit sordid, isn't it?"

"Why sordid?"

"If it wasn't, I'd have thought you would have been a bit more open and honest about it all, brought her with you to meet Mother, the grandmother of her child, when it's born."

"You haven't told her anything, have you?" Geoffrey burst out.

Henry almost grinned. "About your marriage, yes, as you asked me to. About Mary being pregnant, most definitely not. Bad enough having had to break the news of your skulking off to get married like some blasted thief in the night. Mother was utterly shocked and very, very upset. How do you think she'll be when she learns you *had* to get married?"

Geoffrey's lean face clung to its stubborn expression. "I shall tell her. In my own way. In my own good time."

"And when will that be?" Henry's taut shoulders sagged and he drew a cigarette case from the inside pocket of his casual jacket. "Best not leave it too late," he warned through a wreath of smoke as he lit up.

-

William, waiting impatiently for Mary's return after her week away from work, saw it stretch into two and then three. At the end of the third week, growing ever more concerned, he went to her home and knocked on the door.

He knocked several times but there was no reply. Mystified, he walked away, all sorts of reasons for her non-appearance going through his head. Perhaps the conference had taken longer than expected. But surely not this long. And wouldn't she have written to him – a small note at least – telling him what was happening, hopefully saying she couldn't wait to get home and see him? Had she been taken ill? But bad news travels fast and he'd have been told. Had she taken her aunt on holiday? No one had answered the door.

For a short while he contented himself with that possibility, but by the time he reached home it had been swept out of his head as ridiculous. Mary hadn't that kind of money to throw away. She earned better wages than once she had, but it still wasn't all that much – certainly not enough to go away on holidays with – and as well as that, she was saving hard, like himself, so they could get married. Anyway, it was March. Who ever went on holiday in March? And surely she wouldn't have gone without letting him know what she'd intended to do. Something must have gone wrong. Had she had an accident? Was she lying in some hospital way up north? Was she...

With a gasp, William struck that last, foolish thought from his mind. If anything bad had happened, he would have known; everyone would have known. No – it was nothing like that. But it was mysterious, and after the first pangs of anxiety, he began to feel annoyed, then angry. She had no right.

"Don't worry about it," his father said when he confessed his feelings. "It'll all turn out to be nothing at all." But his mother said, "Still, she should have let you know, love. Now come and eat your dinner."

–

"Heard the news, young Goodridge?"

Samson stood before his quarry, legs astride in a posture he always adopted when about to enjoy himself at another's expense.

William, in no good mood with no word yet from Mary, well into her fourth week of absence, gave Chef a belligerent glance as he came into the kitchen to collect an order.

"Heard what?"

"That gel you were sweet on, going around with. I heard she went and got herself married."

"Sorry, Chef?" William took hold of a dish of Duchess potatoes in one hand and one of mixed vegetables in the other. "I haven't got time for games."

Samson ignored his terse reply. "To the boss. Didn't you know?"

Now William stopped, so sharply that he nearly lost his grip on the mixed vegetables. "What're you talking about?"

"About that Mary Owen who used to work here in my kitchen. I s'pose we should call her Mrs Lett now. Mrs Geoffrey Lett."

"This some kind of joke?" But a weight was growing in his chest.

The head chef's grin vanished. He almost appeared sorry at the look on the other's face. "I thought you might've known, young'un. I thought maybe you and her had parted company. You don't talk of her, do you? Anyway" – he brightened a little – "that's the news. Little Mary Owen went off a few weeks ago and has come back Mrs Geoffrey Lett. Sorry if that's been a shock to you, Goodridge. I thought you and her... well, you know. Go and ask someone if you don't believe me."

He wasn't sorry at all, only taken aback, perhaps, by the look William guessed must register on his face, for he felt it himself: blank, cold, flesh stiffening as though in death.

Without a word, William turned, and balancing a dish on the palm of each hand, pushed through the swing doors and into the restaurant.

His body reacting automatically, for his mind seemed incapable of thinking, he went through the process of serving and clearing away, moving to the beck and call of diners though his ears hardly heard what was said, merely that requests seemed to be conveying themselves somehow to him.

But Eustace Emmanuel, the head waiter and a very exacting man, wasn't happy, his hands animated. "Hurry. You are far too slow. You dawdle, and we are so busy. Ees it you have a late night last night enjoying yourself? I tell you: you do not perk up, I see you not keeping your position."

Will was normally quick and efficient, and around six weeks ago Emmanuel had recommended he be trained to serve dishes other than vegetables – another small step up the ladder that had overjoyed William, seeing his salary about to rise. Until now, judging by his superior's smile, he had managed to please.

"I'm sorry," William responded, only half his mind on the apology.

"There ees no time for sorries," echoed Emmanuel. "Two wrongs make no rights. So move more quickly, please."

William moved more quickly. Too quickly. Haste coupling with thoughts that remained elsewhere, he spilled a couple of peas into the lap of a lady diner, an actress from a nearby theatre. Fortuitously, she benevolently waved away William's apologies, saying as she flicked the tiny green orbs off a skirt of the same colour, "It's only a pea, dear man, no harm done. I've had worse on me, darling – haven't I, *Edgar?*" The question full of connotation, her escort saw the joke, though not before Emmanuel, his eyes on his trainee the whole time, had taken a more sombre note of this bit of clumsiness.

William's mind returned to the shock of the news about Mary. Hardly able to believe it, telling himself he couldn't believe it and that after work he must seek the truth, he managed to blindly bump into a rather corpulent man pushing his chair back and getting up to seek the gentlemen's toilet. The silver tray of starters destined for another party of diners wobbled precariously. Thankful that it didn't crash to the floor with a clang loud enough to startle the whole vast restaurant, he counted his blessings as the man chuckled heartily and said, "Whoops, me lad!" in a jovial sing-song fashion. "*Nearly* had a fine mess on our hands," he continued and decently allowed him by before getting out.

William, seeing his station head waiter frown, resolved to put all else out of his mind but his job, and realised he hadn't even apologised to the fat man as any good waiter should have done, whether the incident was his or the customer's fault. Again he pulled himself up sternly.

Obviously not sternly enough. Minutes later he fumbled a serving of sole *a la bourguignone* so that the fish broke over the edge of the plate, to the intense irritation of no less than Mrs Pansy Lambert, a regular and much-cherished customer. Wife of Alfred W. Lambert, a well-known money-lender and millionaire, she was not given to a sense of humour, merely a sense of wealth. Unlike the jolly, rather voluptuous actress with the peas, the voice of the millionaire's wife shrilled angrily across the restaurant, causing other diners to pause in their conversation and crane their necks towards the suddenly raised voice.

"My God, man! I don't want *that* now. Take the thing away."

"I do beg your pardon, madam," William said a little too tersely. After all, the broken end of fish hadn't touched the table, merely hung over the rim of the plate, if dangerously close to the cloth. Quickly he leaned forward, and with a deft touch of the serving fork and spoon, in a split second had tipped the offending piece of fish neatly back to the centre of the plate.

The woman's voice rose to a shriek.

"What do you think you are doing? Do you expect me to eat this now it has been manhandled by you, you silly man? Fetch me your head waiter."

William straightened. "I'm very sorry, madam."

It didn't come out as it should have. It was terse. He could hear it himself. He was letting his private feelings show, something unforgivable in any waiter. He was expected to be cheerful and willing without being too servile, but somehow sharpness had crept into his reply, and all that kept going through his head was: Stupid woman, making such a bloody fuss about a piece of broken fish. A bit of money, they think themselves God's own neighbours.

He caught himself retorting, "There's nothing wrong with it, madam." Unforgivable.

"Nothing…? *Nothing*…" The middle-aged, lightly made-up cheeks began to flare under their dusting of face powder. "How dare you — a mere employee of this establishment — address me in that way? Never have I been spoken to so rudely in all my life, and from a *waiter*! I wish to see the *maitre d'hôtel*. Immediately. I wish to see Mr Henderson. Or Mr Lett, if he is about."

Fortunately, so William thought as his heart pounded rapidly enough to make him feel somewhat sick, neither Lett brother was about. Even so, rudeness to a customer, especially such an important customer as Mrs Alfred Lambert, would not go without punishment, even dismissal. He dared not think about it.

Mr Henderson was already at his side, his hands clasped in readiness to humble himself before his valued customer and apologise profusely, taking the blame upon himself for allowing one of his staff to make her ill at ease and, perhaps, spoil her whole day. But first he snarled at William from the corner of his mouth, none other but William hearing or seeing, "Get out! Now!"

-

William stood in the small office off the kitchen while Henderson, the *maitre d'hôtel*, confronted him with a cold blue stare, having already prepared his dressing-down.

"What the bloody hell did you think you was doing?" A voice vastly different to the well-spoken accent he presented to his customers. "I want no explanations," he continued as William attempted to speak. "And I don't intend to give you no prior warning. Your station head waiter was watching the bloody mess you was getting yourself into this evening. We can't have it. Not from no one. And certainly not from someone he's been trying to train up. Well, you took advantage and I want no excuses. You're out, Goodridge. Out on your bloody ear. This place ain't going to lose it's good name over one damned stupid waiter. You can draw what's owing to you. It's a shame. You was shaping up good and all. But uncalled-for rudeness we won't tolerate."

William felt desperation flowing over him, worse even than that he'd felt while waiting for his telling-off. All along he had guessed his conduct would call for no less than dismissal, but now it was coming about, he saw all his ambitions lying in ruins – those which Mary had not already ground into the dirt, and he still couldn't believe that news, let alone this.

"I'm very very sorry, Mr Henderson." Was he reduced to begging the man? "It won't happen again. I've got a deep private worry—"

"I don't care about your bloody deep private worry," interrupted Henderson. "This is a job,

Goodridge, what calls for *acting*. Like actors on a stage. The show must go on. What would happen to the audience if an actor *showed* he was grieving or something? It's his job to keep his audience's interest in the play or whatever, not stand there airing his bloody personal feelings and grudges and worries. You've upset a valued customer and I won't have it. I don't care what you're upset about. How do I know it won't happen again, the next time you feel a bit put out?"

"I swear it won't happen again." It hit him hard, this having to plead, worse as Henderson gave an acid chuckle.

"I ain't going to give it a chance to. I'm sorry, Goodridge, this was too serious to let go of. I'm dismissing you."

There was no point arguing. Besides, he had his pride. He was aware of faces watching him from the kitchen as he made his departure, and was sure that among them was the head chef with his grinning features. He would not look back to see. He heard the rear door close after him to keep out the March wind as he walked away. Without warning he was a man without a job, one more added to the lengthening dole queues, and without even a reference; a man betrayed by the girl he thought had loved him; a man full of grief at what she had done – if it was true – and, if it *was* true, hating her, the world, and himself.

It was true. Mary had married one of the Lett brothers. Geoffrey Lett. The man had pursued her, courted her, flattered her until he had turned her head and then had married her. Will didn't need to be told all this. Silence from Mary was all he needed. If only she'd had the courtesy to write to him, he would perhaps have forgiven her. But not a word. He could understand her falling in love with someone other than him. It happened. Some of the anger – it had not even really been anger, he told himself – had diminished, though it wasn't easy not to feel pain. If only she had written and explained. Surely she must have known she owed him that.

–

It was proving so difficult trying to write this letter, as though each stroke of the pen was being imbedded into her own flesh.

She sat by her bureau in the flat Geoffrey had got her. It was so quiet here, overlooking the trees in the park, the street below hardly trodden by feet and only the occasional motor car passing by. It was a beautifully furnished flat – a *pied-a-terre*, Geoffrey had called it, because he said that they would eventually find themselves a lovely house, and meantime this would be their love nest.

But Geoffrey wasn't here at the moment. He was at his mother's home in Essex – perhaps telling her about their marriage, Mary hoped, letting her down lightly because he'd said she wouldn't be too pleased about not being told beforehand and would feel left out. So now, while she was on her own, was the time to write to William to try to explain the suddenness of her actions.

It wasn't my fault, she had written. *I was taken by surprise as much as anyone.* Moments later, because the words struck her as so hackneyed, she had torn it up and started afresh.

The second attempt was no better. Now she sat before another clean sheet, staring down at it, her mind seething with words to say yet blank to all those she ought to be saying.

She hadn't told Geoffrey she was writing to William. She'd mentioned that she ought to but he had advised against it.

"You'll only be rubbing salt into the wound," he'd said. "That's if there's any wound to rub salt into."

At the time it had echoed her own opinion that she and William had hardly been what people might call going steady, even though they been going out together for quite some time. They hadn't even become engaged, and if she was truthful she had never felt anywhere near engaged. William was a lovely person, gentle and kind; the girl he eventually married would have a husband in a million, but if the love she felt for him had been the same as that which she now felt for Geoffrey, she would have waited. There had been a spark at one time, but with talk of marriage always being put off, that spark hadn't really developed into a flame. Yet she had loved William in a way, and probably, if Geoffrey hadn't come along...

Mary quickly bent her head over the new sheet of paper and began rapidly to pen more words, but then studied what she'd written and with an explosive breath of irritation snatched up the expensive blue bond to screw it into a stiff ball and drop it among the rest of the spoiled paper in the little wickerwork waste-paper basket at her feet.

"Oh, William. What do I say to you?" she asked of yet another fresh sheet. "How do I explain all this and not hurt you? I don't want to hurt you."

She was going to have to tell him sometime. She owed him that. But how do you vindicate a step that can only cause pain to another? And how many excuses are enough to take away the pain of rejection? Yet not writing or confronting him, wasn't that worse? How must he be feeling right now, not hearing from her, or worse, hearing it all from someone else?

Gripping the fountain pen hard, she withdrew another clean sheet of paper from its shelf and bent her head to apply herself to the task in hand, this time with more determination.

Dear William...

The pen seemed to stop as of its own accord. The words she had been about to write now sounded so trite that Mary flung the pen down in fury. On impact, a shiny blob of rich blue-black ink leaked from the nib like a thick exclamation mark straight across the word "Dear".

"I can't!" she cried aloud to the quiet flat. "I don't know what to say."

Anything she said would only make matters worse. *It all happened so quickly.* How would that help to assuage hurt pride, sense of loss, of losing the girl you love to another man, being defeated by him? *I was so carried away by all that happened to me.* How charming it would be to read such a statement.

But she *had* been carried away, or had let herself be carried away, dazzled by the marvels she had been shown, dazzled by Geoffrey's attentions – and then, just as she'd been laid low, realising herself pregnant, he'd come to her rescue, had married her, gallant and loving, and she had desired him. And now, all full of remorse towards the man she had betrayed, what words could soften that blow she was surely delivering to William's stomach?

Geoffrey had said that what was done was done and nothing could undo it. But he wasn't the one who had to tell the man whose back she had stabbed about her new-found love. Any apology could only be an insult.

Sadly she gave up trying. Perhaps tomorrow she'd find the words.

William sat at home that third day with no motivation to go looking for work, under his mother's feet as she went about her housework. She had told him it was no good mooning about. She had liked Mary but on reflection had always felt a little sneaky concern regarding her.

"Too ambitious, that one," she said. "I always felt she'd finally go flitting off to new pastures. You just 'ave ter put it all behind you, love. Pull yerself together and look for work. There must be something out there for you."

It all went over his head, or rather he closed his mind to it, for he had no stomach for his mother's truths about Mary. He sank his nose deeper into the *News Chronicle* which his father had forgotten to take with him to work and made no reply. His mother didn't even notice.

"It's not as if you ain't got a trade, love." Busy sweeping the parlour lino ready for mopping, she tapped his feet with the broom and he lifted them up so she could manoevre it beneath them. "I do wish you'd get out from under my feet. I know you was dismissed for being rude to a customer, but I expect the stuck-up old bitch deserved it. They think they've every right, but waiters are people too. You don't 'ave to 'ave a reference for every blessed restaurant. It weren't as if you was dishonest. Some place will take you on. And your dad's making enquiries at his firm as well, so don't lose heart, son. Something'll turn up soon. Though it won't if you don't go looking. It ain't going to leap into your lap on its own."

William just let her chatter on. Whether it turned up or not, he had no heart to stir himself looking. But what did turn up he wasn't at all prepared for. Around lunchtime the following day there came a knock at the door.

"Probably the insurance man," said his mother. "Go and answer it for me, love, while I go and get me purse."

He took his time about putting aside the crossword he'd been doing in yesterday's *News Chronicle*, his father having remembered to take this morning's with him, and eventually his mother tutted impatiently and went to the door herself. She came back, her expression concerned, behind her a figure whom William could not discern in the darkness of the windowless passage.

"Will, love, it's… it's your boss."

Will looked from her to the shadowy shape. "My boss?"

"One of 'em."

The figure detached itself from the gloom of the passage and William drew in a sharp breath. "Mr Lett."

Henry Lett stepped forward. He held his trilby in his hand, and it gave him such a humble appearance that William's first thoughts flew to Mary. For

Henry Lett to come here, it could only be bad news. His heart began to race sickeningly at Henry Lett's opening words.

"William, I hope you don't mind this intrusion."

He wasn't listening. "What's wrong? What's happened?"

"Nothing is wrong, William." Unlike all others at Letts, he called all his lesser employees by their first name. "Except that I haven't been at the restaurant for a few days, so I had no idea you had been dismissed."

Nothing about Mary, at least nothing grievous. Relief was like a flood of warmth through his veins. His mind more rational, he supposed the man had probably taken pity on him and intended giving him a reference after all. Henry Lett was a fair-minded man in all things. Though why the need to come in person? Guilt? Well he could stick his guilt where it hurt most. As William felt at this moment, dismissed out of hand, his pride wounded, he wouldn't lower himself to doff a cap and take Letts' reference if it was handed him on a gold platter. He would get by without it, thank you very much!

"I was dismayed to hear what happened," Henry Lett was saying. "I've had my eye on you, William, as worthy of promotion in time."

Well, he was too late. William's lips tightened as he stared out the man. His mother was begging Mr Lett to sit himself down, and asking would he like a cup of tea, in response to which invitation their guest expressed his thanks but said he would have to be on his way as soon as he had finished talking to her son. Looking disappointed, she left them alone, their visitor coming straight to the point.

"To make it brief, William, I'm here to apologise for the way in which you were dismissed. You're a good worker, always cheerful and willing, and I know you are spoken well of by many of our customers. It must have been something very important for you lose sight of yourself the other evening. Although" – a wry twitch stretched the right corner of his broad lips – "I happen to know of that particular lady. Bit of a battle-axe – and a bit of a snob – who doesn't realise that my father knew of her beginnings…" Catching himself verging on tittle-tattling, his lips straightened then softened again. "You have my sympathy, William." Now he became completely sombre.

"I've come here firstly to say that I want to offer you your position back, as I highly value your work. And also, since I imagine the reason for your conduct must have been quite serious, to ask if there is any way in which I can help."

William was flabbergasted; could only shake his head violently. He had no desire to display his private woes to the world, least of all Mr Lett. But the man could not leave, having seen the bleakness that lay in the gesture.

"May I hazard a guess?" he asked, and, without waiting for a response, continued, "I believe you were walking out with a certain young lady, Mary Owen." Again he did not pause for a reply. "I take it you heard about she and my brother, and that the subsequent shock would have been behind your quite uncharacteristic attitude the other day. Did she give you no warning, by letter perhaps?"

William shook his head glumly, glad his mother wasn't in the room to witness this tearing down of his resolve.

Henry Lett's expression had become full of concern, though in some odd way it did not seem to be entirely directed at Will as he went on speaking.

"It was a shock. To me, to all of us. My mother is devastated. He said nothing of what he was about to do. And I... My dear man, I know how you are feeling. I'm ashamed to say that you and my brother weren't the only ones to feel a particular attraction towards Mary Owen. Though knowing that you and she... Had it been me, I wouldn't have taken her from you, William. Had it been me, I'd have hoped that in time you and she might have decided you were not destined for each other after all, leaving the way clear for the honourable attentions of another. I'm afraid my brother had no such qualms. He and she were already—"

"He had no damned right!" William broke in, making no effort to curb the outburst. "I'm sorry, Mr Lett, I have to say it. He had no damned right. Mary was my girl. He knew that. He must have known. She would have told him."

But would she? He fell silent, knowing that she obviously hadn't, and his bitterness deepened.

The silence between the two men was beginning to stretch to breaking point. It was William who broke it, his heart now truly on his sleeve, his misery complete for having given tongue to it.

"It doesn't matter whether she told him or not. They're married now. I can only wish her happiness, that's all. I can see how a girl's head can be turned by a good-looking, well-off chap like him. If it hadn't been him, it would have been someone else rich, I expect. But I never thought she was that kind of girl, to go after money. It just shows how wrong you can be." This last he said with deep acrimony.

He saw Henry chew at his lip, as though arriving at a painful decision. "Please, don't blame her. I think she would have gone back to you if it hadn't been for... William, I think you deserve to be told the truth. The truth is, Mary *had* to get married."

"Had?" The word did not entirely penetrate.

"Surely you know what I'm saying." It appeared difficult for Henry to form the words, as if he were being forced to eat a handful of salt.

William's eyes narrowed as the significance of that word "had" became apparent. There seemed no more to be said, yet Henry had more to say.

"Apart from myself, and of course my brother, you are the only one to know about it. I tell you because I don't want you to think Mary a gold-digger. She was never that. I think she was flattered by his attentions. Perhaps, to a girl like her, money did seem attractive. Geoffrey is a man about town for all he's only just twenty-one. She got carried away and then found herself in a condition she would rather not have been in.

"I think at first Geoffrey wanted her to get rid of it, but when she couldn't bring herself to do that he married her. God knows why. I must say this for him, some would have washed their hands of her, but he didn't. The only wrong thing he did was to go off and marry her without telling anyone. He has hurt his mother and enraged his sisters. But no one except myself, and now you, knows the reason why he married her."

"They'll all know eventually," William said, astonished that he could sound so calm. In reality he felt dead.

"Yes." Henry was looking reflectively at the floor, seemed to be talking to himself, a sad ring to his tone. "Mother will never receive her. I'm sorry to say she will always blame her daughter-in-law rather than her son. To her mind he will have been entrapped by a scheming hussy. But Mary doesn't yet know what lies in store for her. If she does imagine her life from now on to be a bed of roses, I'm sorry to say she will be in for bitter disappointment. Had she turned her eyes on me, for instance, I'd have done my damnedest to seek my mother's approval before ever asking her to marry me. I'd have looked after her and she wouldn't have *had* to get married."

William was looking hard at him, a cold feeling in his eyes. The man was talking as though he wasn't here, as though he didn't feature in this matter.

"Had she married *me*," he said sharply, "she'd have been on her home ground, among her own kind. People like you are ruinous to people like us."

He expected the man to look up angrily, to tell him to watch his words, but Henry Lett didn't. He remained staring at the floor, and when he spoke, his voice shook and his tone suggested an exact echo of what William was feeling.

"Yes. Like you, I am worried for her. I only hope my brother treats her with the consideration due to her by a husband. It's the reason why I need you to come back, William."

He did not say "want", he had said "need". Now he looked up suddenly and appeared surprised at the unyielding look on William's face. With a visible effort, he smiled at his employee.

"If you do, I shall see that you will never be looked down upon – not by me, not by my brother, nor by Mary herself. It's all I can do to make amends for what he has done, for what I – anyone – might have done given half the chance." He was gazing unwaveringly at William.

William's eyes narrowed.

"What you mean is, if she'd looked at you instead of your brother. I expect you too would've had no qualms about enticing her away from me if you'd got in first?"

Henry was biting at the inside of his cheek, appeared uncomfortable. "Not in the same way as he. I wouldn't have taken advantage of her."

"Why not?"

He seemed taken aback by the directness of the question, which almost had the form of an accusation. He made a little sound of clearing his throat. "I respect her too much to do a thing like that. I would have been decent to her, a friend to her."

William let out an explosive grunt of derision. "Huh!"

"That's the truth. I would never have betrayed her trust."

He seemed uncertain of himself, as would a man who knew himself to be lying and loathing it. At first, William heard the word "friend" as pure deceit; thought that Henry would have been no friend at all to Mary, would have but helped himself to all he could get, just as his vile brother had. It came as a shock to realise that although Henry *was* lying, it was in a different context; that when he'd said, "I would have been a friend to her," what he was really saying was, "I'd do her no wrong for I am in love with her far too much," though it would have been beyond his capacity to lay his heart on his sleeve outright.

In that second realisation he knew that they were both equally in love with Mary, was suddenly aware of

Henry's feelings for her as Henry was of his. Two men equally desolate became one in their desolation, both resolving to see that she came to no harm, should harm be afoot.

Slowly and deliberately William nodded. "Yes, Mr Henry. I'll go back."

He felt the breath come into his lungs. Loathing Geoffrey Lett as he did, bitter as he was towards the girl who'd betrayed him, all his common sense told him he should give the job a wide berth, put it all behind him and seek work elsewhere, far away from Letts. But a stubborn reaction, a bloody-mindedness had come over him. He'd take Henry Lett's offer. Henry Lett, being full of guilt, would do all in his power to give William promotion, but he would rise to the top by his own merits; he didn't need Henry Lett's help or anyone else's in order to do so. Ultimately he would show Mary that she had chosen the wrong man.

Thirteen

In a way life couldn't have been more wonderful. In another it couldn't have been more dull. Wonderful because she was Geoffrey's wife and he loved her. Dull because for months, except for a couple of times, she had hardly been anywhere or met anyone.

Five months since that wonderful honeymooon to New York and back, and she had been just once to the theatre – in a box for just the two of them – and once, on the first of April, to watch the Oxford-Cambridge Boat Race from a launch owned by a friend of Geoffrey's, with a party planned for afterwards. It was then, as they got in the car to drive off to Putney, that he noticed how even her rather loose summery dress could no longer conceal her bump when a light breeze blew the material against her form.

Unable to get out of the arrangements he had made several weeks before, he had got her to put on an all-enveloping winter coat despite the day, forbidding her to take it off. There had been a cool breeze on the river so that she had needed the coat, but his attitude had hurt and annoyed her and, sulking, she hadn't spoken to him for the rest of the day. They had come home before the party, not because they weren't speaking but because he knew she would have had to take her coat off.

That night he had suggested it would be best they stay out of the limelight until the baby was born. Still furious with him, she had to admit he was right. No one knew of her condition; no one could count on their fingers and come to the obvious conclusion; so far no newspaper had got wind of it – and although it wouldn't have made blazing headlines, people that mattered could read even a two-inch column stuck in some comer of page eight or nine of the society pages, and neither of them wanted that. It would be as they had planned. As soon as she recovered from having the baby they would go out and about, giving people to believe that she had not been well for some time. After a year or two, hopefully, no one would query a small child's presence. In fact, who ever needed to see a small child? Children not only should not be heard, there was little cause for them to be seen either. Few of their society friends ever showed any interest in small children; if any of them had offspring, they too kept them in the background.

Life, nevertheless, was good, even if she didn't see Geoffrey every day of the week. The spacious luxury flat he'd chosen in West London as far away from his mother's home as he could possibly get without deserting the capital altogether, overlooked

Kew Gardens. She had been able to take walks there as summer approached, with Geoffrey when he was there, or alone when he wasn't. Sometimes her personal maid, Sarah, who had become more like a friend than an employee, would go with her.

Geoffrey had engaged her the day he'd installed Mary in the flat, together with a cook, Mrs Divers, and a woman who came in three times a week to do the heavier cleaning, a Mrs Hutchings, one of the many thousands of war widows who now needed to earn a living. She was a pathetic soul, giving to bemoaning her own lot, the ever growing dole queues, and how her "poor Albert" had given his life for nothing. "War fit for heroes?" she would query acrimoniously. "Some hopes!"

Mrs Divers, a plump woman of about fifty, was also a war widow but kept herself to herself – Mary didn't even know her deceased husband's name or where he had been killed. Luckily for Mary, she had no wish to know anything about her employer's wife, was of the old school of domestics and looked askance at the bond which had developed between mistress and maid. She would drop a prim curtsy whenever Mary entered the kitchen tucked away at the end of a passage, would accept the menu she insisted Mary compose, and go briefly over the accounts with her. Otherwise Mary never set eyes on her.

Today Mary sat alone in the rather large sitting-room. It was a little too large for her taste so that she always felt lost in it when she was on her own. She felt despondent. Probably the imminent birth, she thought; there was just under a week to go, with an expensive nurse due to come in tomorrow and an equally costly doctor on call.

This sense of waiting wasn't particularly thrilling; she merely wished it was all over and done with. For all she wasn't as huge as she'd imagined she would be, it was as though a tight football lay inside her, pushing out her navel until it looked like an appendage – a football incessantly on the move and changing shape as unseen limbs pushed and kicked at her body. Her abdomen appeared to have a life of its own, causing her to suffer endless bouts of heartburn and stretching the skin, threatening her with those silvery stretch marks Sarah told her some women retained after a pregnancy. So far she could see none when she looked at herself in the minor, but that didn't guarantee there wouldn't be any.

She prayed not as she sat on her own – it being Sarah's day off – with nothing to do but read, and she was sick of reading. She hadn't knitted, for why bother when Geoffrey gave her money enough to buy everything the baby would need? Nor did she feel particular excitement about the coming birth; more fear, and this wish for everything to be over with and back to normal. Perhaps once it was bom, when she saw it as a person and not as a squirming lump, she would want to cuddle it and think of it as her own.

It had been a long wait. August almost over, summer almost gone, there had been little to do except go for walks. It was Thursday. Tomorrow Geoffrey would be home. He was planning to stay until the birth before showing himself in the restaurant – a mere formality, for apparently Henry was there most of the time, dedicated to the place as he was. It was doing famously, she'd been told, both brothers in with all the distinguished names: illustrious stage stars, well-known film stars, prominent theatre owners, imminent bankers, Members of Parliament, titled heads, and also, Geoffrey told her darkly, a good few shady characters. "Henry knows them better than I," he told her after he'd made her laugh about some of their doings. "But he's always been hand in glove with most of the clients."

In some ways she missed the place, the office, the old excitement of the restaurant. Maybe it was because she was lacking excitement herself. When the baby arrived, a nurse hired for it, after a suitable lapse of time, Geoffrey would take her back to see the place. Then she would be wife of one of the owners, a totally different role.

Out of the blue the face of William flashed before her and she wondered did he still work there. Geoffrey had never said. Why should he? She'd never asked. A tiny surge of regret went through her like low fleeting pain, gone in a flash. There was no reason for regret. They'd not been engaged, not officially. He'd probably found another girl, even become engaged to her. Again a small stab, this time akin to jealousy, though why she should be envious she didn't knew; it was pointless, when she had everything. Everything, she thought, with the dull ache returning, but recognition in society – she still hidden away here – and acceptance by Geoffrey's mother, refusing to acknowlege her still. That more than anything caused her pain.

–

Having kissed Mary goodbye on Wednesday, saying he'd be home again by Friday night, Geoffrey went to the restaurant to show willing. But there was little for him to do. Henry was well in charge, chatting with customers who mattered for all the restaurant manager was there too, and had already gone through the kitchen accounts with Samson while keeping an eye on the staff to be sure all was going smoothly.

He greeted Geoffrey off-handedly almost, hardly making time to speak to him except to mention that so far this year banqueting bookings were up again, to around 11,221, which, he remarked, was excellent. He then carried on enquiring after various diners' welfare and whether they were satisfied with the service, which they invariably were.

Geoffrey felt insignificant. True, he too had been warmly greeted by several he knew as he made his appearance: Lord Birkenhead with around twenty guests, Lord Thomson with a party of fifteen; Arnold Reeves, one of the great English hoteliers, on whose launch Geoffrey and Mary had been guests in April, now sitting with friends and bellowing at Geoffrey, "How's the wife, old boy? Ain't seen her around lately," which put Geoffrey in a stew so that he was forced to make a prudent but hasty retreat.

He went and visited his mother again to beg her to recognise Mary after all this time. She refused flatly, saying that as she hadn't been consulted about his choice of a wife, it was a little too late – wasn't it? – to expect her to be gracious to the woman.

"My advice is for you to free yourself of this unsavoury marriage and seek a divorce," was all she'd say. "Find yourself a wife of your own kind and go through the proper protocol of introduction for my inspection, and I shall then feel better inclined towards the new one."

As she still knew nothing of the imminent birth of his child, he bit his tongue and refrained from saying that as he loved Mary he would hardly consider divorcing her, not even on the wish of the king of England. It did cross his mind that he ought to tell her of the situation. Maybe she'd feel differently, knowing she was about to become a grandmother. He wondered how on earth he could break the news, as he would have to do one day. He should have told her at the outset. Then he wondered why he should even care. He and Mother were worlds apart, had never been close, she a cold fish. It wasn't a close family. He hardly saw his sisters, both married. His father had been unloving… well, loving enough with female servants – though Mother had put a stop to that – but towards his children, not at all.

So Geoffrey did not tell her of the baby but returned to London, again feeling aimless and as though he were in Henry's way. He no longer felt part of the business, merely received a share of the profits when they fell due. The honeymoon and the subsequent renting of the flat had been a drain on his pocket. He'd gone to Henry for help but had received only the curt remark, "Who's fault's that?" So he was still having to make ends meet, though entertainment expenses were hardly at a premium with Mary unable to go out anywhere and that had helped a little. He was slowly building up again and thanked God the business was doing well. More than well, judging by this Friday evening: the place packed, several private banquets being held with wealthy customers spending as though money was going out of fashion. Not bad at all. By the time Mary came out of confinement, there'd be money enough and more to go out and about again.

"Mr Lett, sir, a telephone call for you."

The receptionist, a middle-aged woman – the only woman on the restaurant staff, a thin, plain figure made more presentable by a dash of powder and rouge and a smart grey-and-blue uniform dress – stood before him with an expectant expression on her face.

"Thank you," he replied absently and followed her, still thinking of the business and Henry and the cool reception his brother had given him on both visits.

Picking up the receiver, he said, "Hullo?" and heard a man's deep, authoritative voice.

"Mr Geoffrey Lett?"

"Yes?"

"I hoped to catch you there, Mr Lett. This is Dr Aloysius Posford."

Having secured the man to attend Mary when her moment came, Geoffrey felt a small prickle of excitement following the initial shock. His stomach knotting, he heard Posford continue, "Your wife went into labour earlier than expected. She is asking for you."

"I'll come home at once," Geoffrey shouted down the phone, hanging it up in panic, missing the hook and having to make two more attempts before finding it. He went to find Henry who was taking a few moments away from the clamour of diners, leaving the entertainment to his restaurant manager.

"Oh, God!" Henry responded, immediately at one with his brother. "Is she all right? Is there anything I can do?"

"No, it seems she's fine. The doctor's with her. That was him on the telephone and he didn't sound worried. The nurse I engaged is with her too. She's in good hands, but I must go home straight away to be with her."

"Of course. If there's anything – anything at all – you will let me know."

"Thanks, Henry, but it'll be all right. I'll telephone you, let you know the moment it arrives and if it's a boy or girl."

He had never seen Henry so concerned, never felt him so close in spirit. Maybe it would bring his mother closer too, needing to see this first child of her youngest son. She had other grandchildren – his oldest sister had produced two, though his other sister had been married only six months. But he was Mother's youngest son. Surely she would relent now.

–

Mary lay propped up in bed, her daughter in her arms. It had been so quick that she could hardly believe it herself. There had been no need at all for Dr Posford – although having been paid an exorbitant fee for his services, it was right he be present.

It seemed such a short time ago that the nurse had been telling her that she'd forget her pain once her baby lay in her arms. There had been pain; she had cried out for relief.

She had been afraid, remembering that there had been no movement from the baby all day yesterday and during labour, that it must have died. The nurse said it was merely resting for the hard work ahead, and no sooner had that been said than she had been told urgently to "push!" She had been sure her veins would burst with the effort, but moments later had come a flood of something wet, a slithering, and there it was, the nurse saying afterwards, laughing as she put the cleaned and wrapped baby into Mary's arms, that if she hadn't been there to catch it, it might have hit its head on the bottom bed rail, it had shot out so fast.

Told now that her husband was downstairs, Mary gave a shriek of joy and the baby jerked with shock, her tiny arms instinctively coming up as though to catch hold of something.

"Oh, please have him come up. I want him to see his daughter."

The nurse smiled indulgently. The father was already on his way up, could be heard taking the stairs two at a time.

He came into the room and Mary smiled at him from the bed, very proud of her work.

"Darling, are you all right?" He was leaning over her, attentive, would have held her close but for the baby there. Mary gave a triumphant giggle.

"I'm fine," she told him. "No trouble at all. It was so quick. I was terribly brave."

"Of course you were, my love."

"And this is your daughter. Say hullo to her."

He moved back as though stung, then, as she moved the shawl back to reveal a round, amazingly smooth little face, he tentatively reached out and touched one tiny hand, which, feeling the warm safe touch, curled about one finger and gripped tight.

"God!" was all he could say for a moment, then looking back at Mary, he carefully leaned over and kissed her gently, rewardingly. "I'm proud of you," he whispered. "So very proud."

Fourteen

The two men stood listening intently.

"Can you hear it?" Henry said, having called William over from his station in the restaurant to join him during a quiet mid-morning period.

This past year Henry had struck up quite a close relationship with him, although William had never sought it. Since Henry Lett's visit to his home in March of last year when he had told him, almost vehemently, that he would see him do well here, he had climbed so fast that it took his breath away. Station head waiter these last ten months – one of several, each of them in charge of six or more tables – was quite a jump from a humble *commis*. It was certainly a huge jump from having been dismissed.

Had it not been for that mystifying visit when Henry had unwittingly allowed him a peep into his feelings for Mary, he might have wondered what the man saw in him to favour him so. But it was obvious Henry was using him to get back at her in some way for marrying his brother, though what he expected to achieve in compelling her to see the worth of the man she'd given up for Geoffrey, William had no clear idea. Unless Henry too was seething that it had been his brother who had claimed her instead of him.

William, for his part, had washed his hands of Mary immediately after Henry had informed him of her marriage. He refused to acknowledge the pain that still lurked, and he hadn't looked at any other girl since. His parents were at a loss to understand why, and he had been obliged to fob them off by saying he was too dedicated to his job to bother with girls at this moment.

"Can you hear it?" Henry persisted when he didn't answer.

William cocked his head, frowning, as Henry went on, "Listen! Can you hear it now? A faint echo of some sort."

Yes he could, just about. The spasmodic conversation of a scattering of customers enjoying mid-morning coffee – the place would be bulging of course by tonight – was rebounding faintly off somewhere or something in the spacious restaurant. Not enough to bother people, he would have thought.

Henry, however, was a stickler for things being just right, unlike his damned brother who would turn up whenever he fancied and pile on the charm as he blithely moved between tables or stood in the foyer like some tall blond god. Customers recognising him would pause to chat or to share a joke, none of them seeing beneath that bloody hedonistic, hail-fellow-well-met charm of his. Then he'd disappear for days on end, to Henry's obvious chagrin.

Henry was equally as popular as his brother though in an entirely different way. People respected him, were happy to open their hearts to him, felt confident he'd guard their little secrets with his life if need be. With his brother they merely loved a good belly laugh. It was a good combination, William supposed grudgingly, customers enjoying the best of both worlds.

Geoffrey wasn't here this evening. Just as well, for he'd have happily chided Henry for making a fuss about a little thing like an imagined echo.

William wasn't sorry on his own account either. He could never feel at ease with Geoffrey around. He did his best to hide his feelings, but every now and again he'd catch Henry watching him and knew that the dark looks he gave Geoffrey Lett hadn't gone unnoticed. Geoffrey, on the other hand, appeared not to see a thing, the self-opinionated tyke! That was all he was – wealthy, self-assured, but as much an unmitigated tyke as the lowliest unemployable street beggar.

The trouble was, the way he felt when Geoffrey Lett was about, with his brilliant laugh and his strutting, made for an atmosphere which wasn't good for the customers, and it was a wonder that Henry hadn't reconsidered his offer to keep him on. There were times he wondered himself why he stayed, but it was really a form of rebellion in not allowing Geoffrey to push him out or see him walk out and thus enjoy even more triumph over him.

"William, where d'you think it's coming from?"

Pulled back to the present by the enquiry, William applied himself to listening intently. Yes, now he could hear a distinct echo of the voices from the tables below the balcony on which the two men stood. From up here it seemed to be all around them. "It's hard to tell," he admitted.

"But what's causing it?" asked Henry in a mystified tone. "It was Lady Matlock who pointed it out yesterday. She said she wasn't too happy eating with the whole place ringing in her ears. I know she prides herself on keen hearing, but I'm not too overjoyed at having a valued customer notice it. I want this place to feel cosy and pleasant. It can't be if it's echoing every damned word that's spoken."

William was already casting an attentive eye around the restaurant: the huge mirrors along one long wall that made the place look even larger; the high, domed ceiling; the balconies that ran along two sides of the place, each supported by a colonnade of four somewhat plain Roman Doric columns, and the wide, short flight of carpeted stairs leading up to the bar and dance floor area. The bar was resplendent with gilt decor and maroon plush stools, and the dance floor, a circular area of dark gleaming hardwood under an imposing chandelier – at the moment unlit - was surrounded by several slim-legged gilt chairs and tables, three or four maroon plush sofas and a few easy chairs. But the echo seemed to emanate from the restaurant area itself.

"Mr Henry," William said, using the polite term for all that they had this past year become quite close. "I think it has to do with those pillars. Plain stonework does tend to throw back noises. That might be the cause."

"Why didn't they do it before?" Henry queried. "They've been there long enough and no one's noticed it until…"

"Lady Matlock pointed it out," William finished for him with a wry grin. Hadn't he too failed to notice until it had been pointed out to him?

Henry didn't smile. To him this was a serious matter. "Well, it mustn't be pointed out again. As soon as one customer notices it, others will automatically. Lady Matlock has only to mention it and they'll all be straining their ears. We can't have that. But we can't take the pillars down. They help support the roof. Shoring it up would cost thousands."

"Why not *paint* them?" William suggested. "A good thick coat of paint would stop any echo. Get a top artist, or several top artists, to each paint a pillar in their own style. Fabric helps too – if it is the stone that's causing the trouble. Paint and fabric would absorb it. Why not do it in this Egyptian style everyone's gone crazy over since the discovery of Tutankhamun's tomb? Every woman you set eyes on these days is dressed like Cleopatra!"

The tomb of the boy Pharaoh, discovered last November by Lord Carnarvon, had revealed an unbelievable treasure trove with promise of an apparently continuous stream of riches still to come. Since then the English had gone wild, consumed by – the papers coining the phrase – "Tutmania". Women wore weird Egyptian-like bangles, Pharaoh-like headbands, feathers and dresses beaded with Egyptian patterns, some actually trying to walk as they imagined those ancients had. People decorated and furnished their homes with anything that looked Egyptian; even household products bore wrappers with hieroglyphics depicting the stylised Egyptian figures found on the wall of the boy king's tomb. It was about time Letts cashed in on the craze.

Henry's eyes gleamed as the idea caught him, in turn stimulating ever more ideas. "We could do the whole place out. I wonder how much would it cost? I'll have to go over some figures with Geoffrey. The place could stand the outlay, I'm sure. It's doing so well. Yes, I wonder."

He was talking to himself. William, now forgotten, prudently returned to his station which he'd left temporarily in charge of a young but promising *commis de rang* who looked mightily relieved to have his station head waiter come back to take over again.

–

"Yes, you're going to have to tell her. That child is a year old; how you've kept it from Mother for so long is beyond me. You can't go on like this."

"I know that!" Geoffrey barked, his hackles rising.

He had come here early, going up to the small private suite above the restaurant where Henry often stayed after a long night entertaining guests, guessing he'd be there this morning after having had a late Saturday night. In fact he'd woken his brother up, hoping for Henry's support in confronting Mother, an unenviable business which he had put off far too long. He hadn't expected Henry to start telling him what he already knew – that he couldn't go on like this.

At first Henry's conversation had been all to do with changing the restaurant's decor. Enthusiastically greeting Geoffrey as he struggled out of bed, he'd gone to the bathroom to relieve himself, all the while talking through the half-open door about Ancient Egyptian styles, asking what did he think and saying that they'd have to discuss costs. It had taken him a while to realise that Geoffrey was here merely looking for Henry's help in paving the way for him before facing Mother, and then it seemed Henry preferred to take him to task himself.

Angered, Geoffrey's instinct was to feign nonchalance.

"Truth is, I don't care any more," he said to the invisible Henry, who could be heard washing rather noisily. "She didn't want to know about my marriage, refuses to meet Mary, so what she doesn't know won't hurt her."

Henry emerged from the bathroom to begin feverishly dressing in casual shirt and trousers. His tone was sharp. "Of course it's going to hurt her, finding out how you've kept her in the dark all this time."

"I told you I don't much care. I'm beginning to change my mind about telling her anything. We've been married one year and four months and she still won't recognise Mary. It's bloody insane. Mary and I are happy. We're having a good time. Why rock the boat?"

And indeed they *were* having a good time. Little Marianne (Mary had insisted on the name Marianne partly because it was so similar to her name and partly because she remembered her weekend in Paris with such affection that a French-sounding name seemed appropriate – "Marianne Lett, it's got a lovely ring to it," she'd said and he had agreed) was no hindrance. They had a full-time nurse, Penelope Ambrose, to look after her, which gave him and Mary all the time they wanted to themselves.

"The longer you leave it" – Henry was occupying himself looking for a tie – "the harder it's going to get."

"That's exactly why I came asking for your help."

Henry stood up, looked at him and nodded. "To make it easy for you."

It was a statement rather than a question. For a moment Geoffrey stared sullenly at him, hating the truth, then, turning, he let himself out of the apartment without another word.

But Henry was right. He must tell Mother. That he and Mary had kept their secret for well over a year was little short of a miracle. Several times they'd had narrow squeaks; on one occasion in May, pushing the perambulator through Kew Gardens for the air, they'd had to turn sharply down another path as he glimpsed a distant familiar face. What if, recognising him, the gossips got to Mother before he did and told her that Mary had been seen pushing a baby carriage?

"We should move further away," he had said at one time, but the flat was so convenient to the West End and everything going on there.

There had been a couple of rather awkward moments at parties, too. Reintegrated into the social circuit, Mary had been asked if she was feeling better. She had burst out unthinkingly, "Oh, it was so quick…"

The woman had blinked. "Quick? Darling, but Geoffrey said you'd been ill for months."

Mary had hastily gathered her wits. "I mean I finally got better quite suddenly," she managed, ignoring the enquiry, "What exactly *was* wrong, dear?"

Most occasions were much the same, with over-inquisitive women asking how she felt and why Geoffrey hadn't let her be seen since their marriage in New York, and remarking on how quaint it was to go all that way just to get married. (They had had to tell people that their marriage had taken place in America to explain away the fact that nobody had been invited.) "And keeping you under wraps for so long, a pretty thing like you, darling. Said you were ill." Time and time again Geoffrey had managed to rescue her, saying it was because she had been rather delicate for a long time after their marriage, ignoring enquiries as to why she should have been. "Something foreign, no doubt," had been the general conclusion to the mystery.

After a while questions grew less, finally dying away. There was no reason for anyone to know about Marianne, her first birthday celebrated quietly, just the three of them and her nurse. Few society couples aired their offspring in public – such a bore – but in time it would be made known they had a child and no one would be counting – too busy enjoying themselves. As yet Geoffrey still had no wish to rock the boat, but Henry was right. He'd have to tell Mother before she heard it elsewhere.

That was if she was at all interested, he thought resentfully as he made his way back down the stairs and along the passage behind the restaurant, aware of the staff arriving, the head chef's voice dominating, Mr Samson always the first in the kitchen.

–

Geoffrey had decided Mary should be with him when he saw his mother. She was instantly clutched by terror when at the end of September, having let two months go by before telling her of his decision, he sprang it on her one morning in bed.

Her reaction was immediate. "Oh, Geoffrey, no!" The pleasure of lying in late was seeping away. "I can't. That's if she even lets me over the threshold."

"We can hardly have the door closed in our faces if we just turn up," he consoled, his tone light. "Once she sees you, she'll like you." But Mary was far from certain. The happy life she'd grown accustomed to, his mother a mere tiny cloud on the horizon, now threatened to fall about her ears.

These past months had been so wonderful, and she had fallen into it quite naturally as if having known nothing else but a life she'd never have dreamed two years ago of having. Parties, theatres, Headingly, Wimbledon's Centre Court, Ascot, Covent Garden Opera House, tennis parties, night-clubs and mingling with high society had all come her way. She had even been included on the exclusive list of guests at Westminster Abbey for the wedding of the Duke of York and Lady Elizabeth Bowes-Lyon last April, the Prince of Wales having included Geoffrey in his own close circle of friends.

Mary had felt like a duchess alighting from the hired limousine, had moved like one in her fantastic Chanel dress bought especially for the occasion as she and Geoffrey entered through the great Gothic entrance to take their seats albeit at the very back of the dim Abbey. But she didn't mind. As a guest of no less than the delicious Prince of Wales who turned the head of every young woman, all hoping he might look in their direction, Mary had felt more than honoured. Not being further included in the royal reception at Buckingham Palace wasn't at all an anti-climax – she felt privileged to at least have been invited to the ceremony.

So many wonderful things had happened this past year. But now came the reckoning, having to meet Geoffrey's formidable mother whom she should have met at the very outset of her relationship with Geoffrey but hadn't due to her condition.

"I need to settle myself down before we go anywhere near her," she told Geoffrey as they got ready on that Saturday morning, when she realised she could no longer wriggle out of it.

He'd have taken her on the Sunday, Geoffrey said, but his mother went to church in the mornings and preferred to lunch alone. Memories of the old family Sunday lunches were painful to her, with her daughters married, her husband dead, her youngest son to her mind a virtual prodigal and her eldest son more often than not living in his apartment above the restaurant. Her afternoon would be taken up having the vicar and like persons to tea, then going to church again for evensong, home to a quiet supper, then to bed early. Her Sundays were sacrosanct, not convenient for receiving any whom she hadn't invited. All this he told Mary with a caustic ring to his tone and she realised he viewed the prospect of facing his mother with her with as much reluctance as she.

"Can we have lunch somewhere before we arrive?" Mary asked.

"We could grab a bite to eat at our restaurant. You might feel more at home there," Geoffrey suggested hopefully, his use of "our restaurant" immediately stifling her nerves with a blanket of pride as she readily agreed.

She hadn't been near there since concocting that story for William Goodridge about having to attend a conference. She wondered if he still worked there. Probably not. Geoffrey never mentioned him and she'd never asked. Dismissing her worry as immaterial, Mary shrugged it off as, finally ready, she and Geoffrey left.

—

William was pleased with himself having deftly prevented a scene, though unsure if he'd done the right thing. Scenes were said not to be good for trade, yet a rousing argument bordering on fisticuffs between a couple of celebrities brought people in for days afterwards, hoping to enjoy a sequel, especially if they were in the public eye and should know better.

To William's mind being in the public eye seemed to exacerbate the pomposity that usually caused these unwarranted scenes when the parties involved should be keeping their heads down. Titled gentlemen with their mistresses; stage idols who needed public adoration rather than condemnation; Members of Parliament needing their constituents' support; all forgot themselves after a few lunchtime tipples or a late-night supper with too much champagne.

This row had arisen when Mr Samuel Woodward, the well-known City banker – a short, stocky, red-faced man, proud of his acid witticisms but not so easily enjoying them when directed at him – had aimed a caustic if jovial remark at an acquaintance on the next table who was entertaining two ladies of the stage, one of them the celebrated Madame Celestine Vollard. The dig had to do with the other being lucky enough to have two for the price of one judging by what had been ordered – expensive jugged hare for the gentleman, Mr Gordon Gilmore, Tory Member of Parliament for Fendle under Stanley Baldwin, as always on Saturdays, with just chicken and salad for the ladies, who no doubt needed to watch their figures. The victim hadn't seen the humour of the jibe.

Throwing down his napkin on to the table he swivelled in his seat to glare at the tormentor. "Exactly what are you insinuating, sir?" he roared.

Woodward let out a deep bellow of laughter.

"Oh, my dear man, no need to go off half cocked. Cocked? A joke?"

"A poor one. And certainly out of order in public. Filthy minds—"

Madame Vollard, a fiery French woman, who had been feeding her toy poodle bits of chicken under the table, intercepted in the contralto singing voice that had made her name. "I do not know you, monsieur, but you are a silly, silly little man."

Woodward glared, joking put aside. "Gilmore, kindly restrain that woman's insults."

"*That woman!*" came the female scream. "I am called *that woman*? Is you who insult. You… British *pig*! I am Madame Vollard, not *that woman!*"

"Yes, restrain yourself," Gilmore said, "or I shall call you a damned filthy-minded blackguard – which you rightly are!"

William, striding from his station desk, was in time to intervene as both men leapt up to take a swing at each other, but not quick enough to prevent jugged hare being knocked all over Madame Vollard's lap. The other young lady leaped clear of the splashes, her long slim legs catching the legs of the chair, tipping it over with an intrusive rattle.

"Sir! Sir!" William attempted to calm the antagonists, risking a chance slam in the face from the already flailing fists, so far none landing on any chin. "This is no way to behave. Please, Mr Gilmore, your guests…" The risk of being flattened by a wayward blow was diminishing. "Your meal has been spilt down Madame's beautiful dress."

Madame Vollard was screaming, "Look at my dress!" Her voice echoed through the whole restaurant, whose customers were now having a whale of a time as onlookers. "It is ruined! Who is to pay for the cleaning bill? It is the fault of the waiter, the silly man! To put Monsieur Gilmore so dangerously close to such an abominable man!"

All the time the little dog had been yapping excitedly. Now it skittered out from under the table as Woodward went to pick up his own fallen chair and deftly nipped him on a convenient wrist.

The man gave a howl. "That's it!" he yelled. "That's the last time I come here. We're leaving. My bill, if you don't mind!" Dragging his napkin from under his chin and his silent wife from her chair, he proceeded to the foyer – thus avoiding waiting for the bill to be brought to him – threw his money on to the counter and, grabbing his wife's hat and wrap and his topper from a straight-faced *commis*, swept from the premises. The other party left soon after, the remaining customers settling down to relish a jolly good recount of the entire invigorating diversion from an otherwise ordinary lunch.

Half an hour after both parties had left, William was still grinning to to himself each time he recollected Madame Vollard's expression, that rouged mouth wide open, eyes bulging in her handsome face as first the jugged hare went down her and then her little dog took a nip from her by the hated enemy, Woodward. Still grinning, William made a mental note not to put those parties near each other ever again, for they would surely return, for all their threats. People always did, Letts being one of the liveliest restaurants in town, especially at night when parties of men about town entertained lady friends to supper and late-night dancing.

Five minutes later William's smile was wiped from his face as he saw two people enter the restaurant, the woman's escort leaving her briefly in the foyer while he spoke to Mr Henry who'd come down from his private flat to have the earlier incident related to him by the restaurant manager.

The woman stood alone, a little nervous, seeming isolated from those arriving and leaving around her, none of them noticing her. William knew the gentleman, her husband, of course, but her − little remained of the young girl he'd once known. The last time he'd said goodbye to her had been the day she had told him, lied to him, that she had been required to go off to some fictitious seminar to help out with the clerical work. But there had been no seminar − she had slunk off to get married. Not a word to him, not word or sight of her since, not even an apology or an excuse.

He felt the sickness rising up in his stomach, his face turn pale, his lips grow numb. Quickly he turned away and went on with his normal duties. She wasn't going to cost him his job this time; he was too good at it, had worked too hard to gain it – with a little help from Henry Lett of course, with that strange wish to promote him over the heads of others which he still found mystifying.

Fifteen

It still stuck in her mind, like a thorn under the skin, that day Geoffrey had taken her to see his mother. More than twelve months ago and even now the memory caused her to cringe.

It had been a day of trauma right from the very start, seeing William Goodridge, he treating her as just another customer, and then, when she had been too pent up to eat the sole fillets *a la Lyon* she had ordered, hearing him enquire, polite and suave, "Is Madam's lunch not to her taste? Does Madam wish to change her order?"

Polite, yes, but there had been an edge to it – maybe the politeness itself – that had disturbed her so that she had been wretched all the way to Geoffrey's mother's home in Halstead Green, a cold, staid-looking mansion in acres of grounds that had put the fear of God into her from the moment she saw it.

The senior Mrs Lett had been no less cold and staid – enough to have put off Queen Mary herself – with the added advantage of being tall enough to look down on her youngest son's wife, which she had done adequately. Mary still believed that the woman's sole purpose in consenting to meet her had been to mortify her.

They had stayed a mere couple of hours in that frigid, unbending presence but to Mary it had seemed a lifetime and she came away vowing that if she never saw the woman again it would be a blessing.

She often wondered what would have happened had they disclosed Marianne's existence, Geoffrey having forbidden her to mention anything about her. It had hurt, but he had said he needed more time to tell his mother and, as gently as possible, that it was best. She'd have preferred to have seen the evil woman squirm, but it would have been Geoffrey, her son after all, who'd have been hurt, so she had kept her mouth shut.

Geoffrey had eventually told his mother in August, some time after Marianne's second birthday, stupidly assuming she'd give way once she heard about her granddaughter. Instead, there had been a frightful row. He hadn't spoken about it much, but Mary had cried bitterly when he had finally said that his mother had told him that she wanted nothing to do with his "virtual bastard". He'd held Mary close, saying he wanted nothing more to do with his mother himself and suspected her of not being entirely right in the head since his father's death. But it did not help Mary, who now hated the woman with all her heart and soul.

Well, it was all in the past now. Despite being aware of the woman ever hovering in the background, it had been an exciting, eventful year. Henry often came to see her, apparently taking their side in the matter of Marianne. He would spend hours at the flat, whether Geoffrey was there or not, playing with the baby and chatting to Mary. It puzzled her that he seldom seemed to go out anywhere unless on business, appeared always wrapped up with the restaurant as if married to it. Once she asked him why he still hadn't any young lady in tow. After all, he was twenty-six; it was time he should have been married.

He had given her a strange look. "I probably set my sights too high." Then he had laughed, a little hollowly she thought. "There's only one I know who fits the bill, and I can't have her." He had refused to be goaded further by her teasing him about who that might be, and she had finally let it go. But she did enjoy his company. He was so different from Geoffrey in many ways.

Unlike his brother, Geoffrey was full of life, always wanting to be somewhere else. He had filled the whole of 1924 with fun and excitement. He and Mary were seen at so many social events it was said a party wasn't the same without them; his repartee never flagging and always looked for, she hardly missing out any chance to dance, an expert at it to the delight of the opposite sex and the envy of her own as she kicked up her heels to all the latest jazz tunes. They often threw wild and expensive parties in their own spacious flat until it became quite the place to be. Even Prince Edward was seen there on occasion.

New Year's Eve had them celebrating at no less than three separate parties, at one of which she had her first experiment with opium, the odd sensation it gave her leaving her vowing never to try it again though others seemed to enjoy it immensely. But the parties had gone on throughout the year: some wild, some not quite so wild, but most of them eventful and full of excitement one way or another.

One they'd gone to in May had seen Oswald Mosley, the fiery upper-crust ex-Tory MP who had crossed the House soon after Labour won the election, striking up a fierce political argument ending in a fight, with the police having to be called in. Impeccable and unruffled, Mosley had laid an arm about Mary's shoulders, guiding her out before the police began making arrests. He and had then gone back for Geoffrey, his thin lips smirking under that trim moustache of his as he remarked, "No sense in courting trouble" – rather incongruously after having personally started it all – and then departed, as untroubled as if nothing unusual had occurred.

There were so many varied pleasures. They had gone with friends to see Cecil B. De Mille's film *The Ten Commandments*, giggling, behaving more like children than responsible adults, afterwards dancing at a night-club until the small hours. They had invaded Paris for the 1924 Olympics, some of the women Mary knew passing out in the heat though she had revelled in it and Geoffrey had made friends with the muscular American swimmer, Johnny Weismuller, who took three golds for his country and for a while stole her heart.

Paris was the place to be, Paris and London. Paris with the Prince of Wales, being seen in all the smart places. London and concerns about whether there'd be a season or not. She'd become quite used to travelling, to all this night-life, endless cocktail parties, cabaret, horse racing, motoring, motor race meetings, house parties and tennis parties, Ascot and the royal enclosure, where she had bowed as their Majesties passed in their carriage and for which occasion she had bought three exorbitantly priced hats. She and Geoffrey were often in danger of living beyond his income.

Popping off here, popping off there, Mary was no longer worried about slipping into Letts and seeing William Goodridge there when there were so many fine people to mingle with. Geoffrey knew how to attract all the right people; Jackie Coogan hot from Hollywood and treated like royalty; the controversial Noel Coward whose play *The Vortex* was raising so much clamour; famous hostess Mrs Laura Corrigan who had this year sent reply-paid cables from India for her Grand National house party. The list was endless.

But sometimes she longed for a quiet time, just she and Geoffrey and Marianne; Geoffrey putting on gramophone records or just listening to the wireless – still a novelty – but mostly giving some time to

Marianne. She saw too little of her daughter, looked after so well by Penny. Often it didn't seem she was her mother at all, for all that she loved her dearly.

Sitting at her dressing-table making her face up for the Christmas Eve party they were off to, Geoffrey still in the bathroom finishing shaving, she was thinking of Marianne when Penny Ambrose came into the bedroom after knocking and being asked to enter.

Mary turned from the minor, expecting to see Marianne with her, waiting to be kissed goodnight before going off to bed. Instead Penny was alone, her rather plain, square face a little strained.

"Mrs Lett, I think you ought to take a quick peek at Marianne. She's weepy, she wouldn't eat her supper and now she feels hot."

"Hot?" The flat was a little hot, fires in every room against the chill December air outside.

"I mean, she has a slightly high temperature. And she keeps moaning. I don't think she is well, Mrs Lett. It seems to me more than just a cold."

Mary sighed. Penny was a qualified nurse. She should know if Marianne was unwell or not and take the necessary steps. But of course she was doing that, reporting to the mother first.

It was probably nothing at all. So far Marianne had escaped every one of those children's ailments that abounded. Dr Posford, keeping a regular check on her, marvelled that she was always so healthy, even when she had been teething. She usually even escaped colds, and if she did catch one it was soon over. So it was a little shock to hear Penny say she thought Marianne was not well.

"I'll come and have a look at her," Mary said. There was still plenty of time before leaving for the party; it would take about fifteen to twenty minutes to get there in the new Ford. She thought of the midnight-blue dress she would be wearing, bought for the occasion, though she would have to pull in her horns after this. One couldn't just keep on buying new – Geoffrey was getting a little worried about money and Christmas was such an expensive time.

She followed Penny into Marianne's bedroom. Quite large, it doubled as a nursery. She'd said to Geoffrey that they would eventually have to find a house with a proper nursery as Marianne grew older. "And a garden for her to play in." The park was all right, but one couldn't expect her to go there for the rest of her childhood, always with a nurse in charge.

Marianne was sitting on top of the bedclothes, her little lips drawn down, her blue eyes moist, her cheeks bright pink. She looked miserable and was making little high-pitched moaning sounds, as Penny had said. Mary put out a hand and felt her forehead. Warm, not hot, but certainly not right. She bent over her.

"Don't you feel well, darling?"

Marianne shook her head, still too young to describe exactly how she felt, only able to string simple words together.

Mary bent to kiss her cheek. That too felt warm – dry and warm, not natural. Fear took hold of her. She straightened up. "I think we'd best get Dr Posford."

"I think it's only a feverish chill," he said when he came. "You keep this flat too warm, you know. When she goes out, the contrast is a shock."

"We didn't want her to feel cold indoors," Mary excused.

"Mollycoddling," he snorted as he pulled the covers up over the child after examining her. "Cold rooms never hurt anyone so long as one is adequately clothed. Overheated rooms breed germs." He was a man of the old school, apparently frowning on comfort, though Mary suspected he himself enjoyed it well enough judging by the exorbitant fees he charged.

Geoffrey came into the nursery, shaved and dressed in his evening clothes, having taken ages about it so that he hadn't seen Posford's arrival. Geoffrey looked splendid, Mary thought with a small twinge of adoration in her stomach. He also looked worried, finding the doctor here.

"What's wrong? I came to get you, Mary. Is Marianne all right?"

"She picked up a little chill," Mary said. "I thought we should call Dr Posford, just to be sure." She saw a look pass over Geoffrey's eyes and knew he was counting costs again, thinking of the hefty fee for calling Posford out, imagining the man growing fat on unnecessary call-outs. But Marianne's health came first, didn't it?

A small pang of irritation replaced the one of love as Posford said, "Keep her in bed for a few days. She'll be fine."

-

Henry had come home for Christmas. He'd rather have stayed in his penthouse above the restaurant, but Mother had asked him to come. She had asked his sisters and their families who had also responded, though Geoffrey hadn't come. He wouldn't, with Mary not welcome. Had he done so, bringing Mary with him, Mother couldn't with any decency have turned them away, but their stay here would have been miserable. Best they stayed away.

But Henry felt keenly disappointed. How wonderful it would have been with Mary here, if all had been different – a breath of fresh air, she'd have made his Christmas. As it was, though a sizeable enough gathering it was far from a jolly one, maybe because the remaining member of the family wasn't here, certainly because the head of it would never again be.

Christmas dinner, as with Christmas lunch, sumptuous though it was, was quiet. Their mother, never one for talking at table, spoke even less these days. Afterwards she and her daughters repaired to the lounge, she to gaze into the blazing log fire there, they to nibble chestnuts, sip sherry and chat, mostly of old times. Maud's children were sent up to the old nursery to play with their Christmas toys, the menfolk retreating to the library for male conversation, brandies-and-soda and cigars, windows shut against the freezing cold outside. The room reeked of cigar smoke despite Mother's preference to have the windows open at least a fraction in order to help lessen the odour.

Boxing Day was a mirror image of Christmas Day, except that his eldest sister Maud was with her husband's people, making the gathering even smaller and duller. Henry found himself wishing for the solitude of his own flat where he could look out over the rooftops of London and feel the peace of a winter's evening extending way above all the excitement and upheavals of the human race, all looking forward to a new year, 1925, a week from now, with no thought to what trials and tribulations it might bring along with the joys each person hoped for. His excuse that at this particular time of year he should be keeping an eye on the restaurant growing more busy than normal had cut no ice with Mother.

"They can do without you," his mother had said when he mentioned his intention to leave after lunch. "Surely you can trust your own restaurant manager to get along without you being there. That's what you pay him for."

She must have become very out of touch – though she had never really been in touch, except through what her husband had told her – to not even know the name of the restaurant manager, the most senior of their employees. Father had left her a third share in the business but she refused to have anything to do with it; had trustingly, or wearily, handed the running of it to her sons knowing they'd look after her and not wishing to be bothered with business. Her life was here and when Henry mentioned getting back, she was quick to jump.

"I need you here much more, Henry, today of all days. You are the only son I feel I can turn to since we lost your poor father."

"There's Geoffrey?" he said bravely. He saw her lips tighten and knew he had gone too far.

"I hear hardly a word from him these days. I have not closed my doors to him but he behaves as though I have. I cannot speak for his movements. Nor do I wish to."

In the face of this inflexibility Henry didn't feel brave enough to extend the argument a second time round and his mother in turn abruptly changed the subject.

"Henry, when are you going to find yourself a suitable young lady? It bothers me that you are twenty-six and still unmarried. I know little of your private life but surely from time to time you meet *some* nice young ladies."

"I lead a rather quiet life, Mother," he excused himself. "I like it that way."

She looked at him sharply. "Well, you have no business, liking it that way. Not at your age. You should be going out and meeting people – as I suspect your brother does well enough. Too well, I imagine."

"That's his business," Henry said sullenly.

He was dying for a cigarette. He wanted to escape his mother and her awkward questions and go somewhere out of the way for a quiet smoke. But having warmed to her new subject, she seemed loath to let go of it.

"But you *should* be seeing a little life, not staying cooped up in that horrid London flat. You need to begin thinking on your future, marriage – to a girl of some standing who can bring something into the business as well as children."

God, not that again! She had harked on this on and off for the last year or so. Now she was bringing it up again – coupled with the one name she never failed to bring up.

"Young Grace Chamberlain is still unmarried you know. The daughter of one of your father's oldest friends. He still visits to me, the dear kind man, and he and his wife convey me to church in their car every Sunday without fail. If you were here more often you would get to know her much better. She was the loveliest débutante I've seen in a long while, and such a sweet girl. I'm forever amazed that she hasn't yet been swept up by someone."

Yes, he knew her, and she *was* a lovely girl, would have stirred his heart had it not been already touched by Mary. But Mary was married to his brother. He'd have to turn his glances towards someone else one day. Grace Chamberlain could be that someone. Yet something always stopped him.

"Eighteen months since the dear girl came out," his mother went on. "A long time for a young girl to not have a suitor. I'm sure she refuses them because she has her eye on you, Henry."

A discreet tap on the morning-room door interrupted her. Atkinson came in, looking first at his employer then at her son. "There is a telephone call for you, Mr Henry, in the library."

Something about the man's expression alerted Henry's sixth sense that he must not ask in his mother's presence who the caller was. "Thank you," was all he said, and with a small dip of his head towards his mother to excuse himself, hurried out after the butler.

In the hall he asked Atkinson who it was.

"Your brother's wife," came the quiet reply. "She sounded agitated."

Picking up the earpiece balanced on end beside the longstemmed telephone, he put it to his ear and heard Mary's voice. It sounded frantic.

"Is anyone there?"

"It's me, Henry," he replied.

"Oh… Henry…" It sounded as though she was weeping. "I had to ring you. Marianne's in hospital. Geoffrey's there. They say it's diphtheria. She had a cold. At least, we thought it was a cold – Dr Posford said it was – but she was incubating diphtheria and we didn't know. She's so ill. I think she might… I think she's going to… Henry, she's so ill…"

Her words, which had been tumbling out in a continuous gabble so that he could hardly catch all of them, broke off.

"Mary, calm down," he instructed.

By now he himself was hardly calm, his heart racing. "I'll come over. Do you want me to come to the flat or go to straight to the hospital?"

"I'm at the hospital now."

"What one?"

"King Edward's." In a dither she explained where it was, ending, "Henry, please, hurry!"

Returning to the morning-room, his heart thumping like a hammer in his chest, he told his mother. Her expression did not alter except for a rapid blink or two of her eyelids.

"Why should she want you? Her husband is with her. Isn't that enough?"

"I think it's Geoffrey who wants me there," he said hastily, but it did occur to him as he drove that it was strange that Mary should ask him to go to her when she did have Geoffrey there.

The parents were at the bedside when he was shown to the isolation ward where Marianne lay in a single room. Through the glass he saw a tableau that made a stone of his heart – the motionless child's face on the pillow, Mary crumpled over her, Geoffrey with his arm around Mary, his face buried in the nape of her neck.

Neither moved as he went in, the nurse silently closing the door behind him. The air was still and full of the feel of death. There was no need to confirm what he was seeing. Standing to one side, he felt useless, empty, was already weeping inside at Geoffrey and Mary's grief, mostly at Mary's, she so utterly torn down.

He wanted with all his being to take her in his arms and comfort her. But all he could do was stand by, his chest tight with misery.

–

"Mr Goodridge – are you all right?"

William came to himself with young Edwin's voice in his ear. For a moment he stared at the young man as he fought to get his bearings. Good God! Where had he been? He made an effort to smile.

"Yes, of course, lad." His tone sounded strained. "I must have gone off into a world of my own for a moment."

Had it been a moment? Or had he been sitting here in his dream of the past for several minutes? Or had it been several hours? In his mind it had been half a decade. It came as a shock to become aware, not of the genteel clatter of cutlery and the continuous babble of soft voices against a background of soft 1920s music, but the thump of the juke box, the brittle clanking of glasses and harsh, hurried chatter of a busy lunchtime pub.

"I'm sorry to have gone off into a daydream," William said hastily, and smiled. "A fault of age, I expect."

Edwin gestured away the statement, making William realise that the boy had no idea of all that had gone on during that decade. How could he explain? It was important to do so. Perhaps he should try.

It suddenly seemed imperative he did tell him about those days when to the young and wealthy the years had been one long summer and they the gorgeous butterflies that, without concern or under-standing for the less privileged who squirmed below them, flitted here and there in the warmth of their own bright sun, sipping a little of this, a little of that, quite unaware that when their long summer finally died, most butterflies would too.

He had to make Edwin understand – and this time he wouldn't go off into silent reverie but relate how it was, the pitfalls awaiting a butterfly, how they could fall prey to the unexpected, how harshly life could treat even the most privileged, and maybe it was worse for them, for in their acceptance of being privileged they hadn't noticed the traps which the poor always saw looming.

Maybe there was time to explain a little more to Edwin so he would see what a wonderful place Letts had been and could be again, and be taken by it.